D1488356

The Cloister

AUGUST STRINDBERG

The Cloister

edited by
C. G. BJURSTRÖM

Translated and with a Commentary and Notes by
MARY SANDBACH

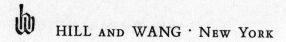 HILL AND WANG · New York

Printed in Great Britain

Contents

I

The Cloister

I

The Cloister

WHEN HE AWOKE in his bed the room was still dark and only two lines of light indicated the position of the window.

But surely he had done as he usually did, gone to sleep with his face away from the light and the window behind the head of the bed. Now his head was by his feet—a not uncommon illusion. In order to put himself to rights he turned his head, and then saw that the window was in its proper place, and that consequently the room must have acquired two windows since the previous day.

This was the day on which he had moved into this hotel room, after having changed his abode five times since he arrived in Berlin. The fact was that he had had no peace of mind since he last turned his back on his fatherland and his family. He had emigrated to Berlin to seek work and a livelihood through his plays.

Now fully awake, and back in his bed after a long excursion as it were, he heard a cock crowing.

"So it's morning! Where was I yesterday? How long have I slept? Three hours at the most!"

Then came baseless anguish of mind, pangs of conscience for no good reason, as he could not remember having done anything actually bad, or made away with any considerable sum of money.

The previous day unfolded itself before him. All its motley events, the part he had played in them, in itself a disgusting, ridiculous and stupid part. He heard every word he had uttered, and felt them all to be tasteless, incautious and crude. He saw every scene . . .

He had ended up in the night den in Friedrichstrasse in company with a young Norwegian dramatist,[1] who had placed a table before him on which were oysters and Rhenish wine. Tired but not drunk he had stretched out on three chairs and talked and talked for hours. He had held forth about the eventful nature of his past life, described scenes, repeated dialogues, analysed them. Speculated about his peculiar fate, which he could not understand; divulged his presentiment of the rise of a new dramatic form, composed a whole play. He had then parted from his friend as if after long and arduous labours.

"You work all the time, even when you're at a tavern," his friend had said. It was the only remark of his he could remember.

The cock crowed again and he thought it odd that they kept fowls at the hotel. Perhaps they were intended for some dinner-party, and Don Juan was now singing his swan-song, in expectation of imminent decapitation. Curious that only these animals end their life by being beheaded, and that they have blood-red combs, and red beards, and spurs on their boots, and treat the dunghill like an occupied fortress, and sing to the rising sun.

Before the night den he had been at a night café, the National, where he had talked to the painted spooks as if they had been gentlewomen. The Norwegian had said—he could hear the words—"How childish you are, talking philosophy to creatures like that. Why do you do it?" "I do it," he now answered, and thought he answered well, "because for me all women are alike."

He was particularly fond of the Café National because it was large and airy and because, in the middle of the hall, there was a fountain that splashed, and in it some goldfish under the palm-trees. For a moment he had turned sentimental and felt sorry for the fishes who were not allowed to sleep. He had tried to

turn off the jet and shade them with a newspaper, but this had
been discouraged.

And the whole time he had talked. "Forgive me for talking
so much," he had said, "but I've not talked for three years,
only babbled."

He heard a drum in the distance. The lines of light grew even
clearer and proved to be the hoops on his trunk. His trunk! The
only bit of flotsam he had left after the great shipwreck, the
only stick of furniture that was his after the auction, the dis-
trainment, the claimants' lawsuits. "And think," he was fond
of saying, "I, who had six rooms plus kitchen, and a holiday
cottage, and a majolica stove, and a painted ceiling, and three
maids, and bells to every room, so that all I had to do was to
push a button and in came punch and soda-water." At the time
everything had to be sold he had thought it was nice to have no
possessions, to be cut adrift from all mundane ties, not to be on
any register, to own nothing but a passport. It made him feel
free and gay. Now he was wandering the world with a trunk
for his servant. He had once adopted the pseudonym "The Son
of a Servant", with nothing more in mind than the fact that his
mother had been in service. But several years later, while pursuing some archaeological studies in the Old Testament, he had
come upon the story of Hagar, and he had read:

"Abraham had two sons, one by his serving maid, he was
borne of the flesh. . . . And he will be a wild man; his hand will
be against every man, and every man's hand against him; and
he shall dwell in the presence of all his brethren. . . .

"And Sarah saw the son of Hagar the Egyptian, which she
had borne unto Abraham, mocking. . . .

"Cast out this bondwoman and her son; for the son of this
bondwoman shall not be heir with my son. . . ."

Had he known this when he characterized himself thus, or
had someone whispered the secret of his fate in his ear? Cast him
out! Yes, that had been the cry, all his life, out! From his home,

from his school, from the community, from his country, from his family. No sooner had he got a roof over himself and them than the cry had come: out! And therefore he had become a hard man, a mocking man! There were those who thought that he had been cast out because he was such a man!

"It's strange," he went on, "that there's no rumble of carts today. Is it Sunday?" He did not know, for he kept no count of the days, did not live in this world, was perfectly capable of writing 1891 instead of 1890, and of putting a question mark after it. Capable of heading a letter Shrove Tuesday or The Dog Days, simply because he did not know the date.

Before going to the Café National he had been to a "Viennese Ball" as an onlooker. He, and a consular secretary, and a doctor[2] had been invited there by an Inspector of Police. It was the most horrible thing he had ever seen. In order that a better check might be kept on them the perverts of the capital had been given permission to hold a fancy-dress ball. When it opened everyone behaved ceremoniously, almost as if they were in a madhouse. Men danced with men, mournfully, with deadly seriousness, as if they were doing something they had been ordered to do, without pleasure, without a smile. Between the dances the couples sat gazing into each other's eyes, as if in them they could read their fate. The one playing the lady's role might have the moustache of a cavalryman and pince-nez, he might be ugly, with coarse, masculine features, and not even a trace of feminity to serve as an apology.

The gods had struck them mad, so that they saw what was not there, were drawn towards what they did not wish and might not have. It was a punishment for unknown sins and certainly not what you would call vice or sensuality, for they looked like outcasts and were incredibly clever at avoiding seeing the Police Inspector and his guests who had seated themselves at a table in the centre of one end of the room, close to which all the couples had to pass. Pandemonium, the seventh circle of Hell, for the unblessed, the wretched, the mentally sick. And they were treated as criminals. The Inspector called them by their Christian names and summoned some of the most interesting among them to his table, so that the author could study them! Some of them approached with funereal faces, unwilling, colourless, and answered evasively. Others were shy, and made childish little gestures, as if they were playing a game.

Most of them appeared to be in love, but in a purely psychic sense. They were bound together by unfathomable sympathy, and the same couples danced every dance together, did not leave each other for an instant, faithful to the death, and jealous. While the ball was in progress the respected old doctor rose in distress and left the table, but returned in a moment still more upset. He had seen his best friend, a highly-placed Civil Servant, whom it was true he had suspected, but without having any proof.

In the female section, where women danced with women, the most noteworthy person was a stately lady, beautiful, distinguished-looking, well-dressed, but not in fancy dress, who conducted herself with the dignity of a lady-in-waiting. Her truly noble features diffused modesty and pain for something, she knew not what, as her eyes followed a radiant young blonde. The Inspector informed them that the two were bound together by a passionate love for each other, and that, as the elder woman was poor, the younger one supported her by selling herself to men she abhorred. Martyrdom here too, self-sacrifice, faithfulness, all the virtues in the midst of vice!

When they left that hell he took with him an impression of something inexplicable, which neither pathology nor psychiatry could explain. It seemed to him that the most horrible thing of all was that everything was done so seriously, and that it was all so respectable!

The room had grown lighter, but there was still no rumble of wheels to be heard. What could this mean? He could tell by his breathing that the sky was overcast, and that the barometer was low. Then, as he inhaled the damp, raw air that tasted of ammonia, he said to himself: "It's snowed during the night."

Once again he began to haul himself up the stream of memory, to find his way back to its source. Before the "Viennese Ball" he had been to dinner with a learned millionaire in the Tiergarten district. He had sat on his hostess's right, and thus enjoyed a certain degree of prestige in that literary-minded family. Wine had flowed, the shoulders of lovely ladies had shimmered between the decanters, the flowers, and the candelabra. After dinner a young beauty, who was related to the family, had engaged him in conversation, but he found her too young and innocent for sophisticated exchanges and soon seized the opportunity to slip away into a small drawing-room. In it sat a solitary lady, fairly young, who looked as if she had been weeping, and kept her lips apart like Madame Staël. She introduced herself as the correspondent of an important newspaper, paid him a compliment, and conversation flowed freely. The lady, to whose appearance he paid no attention, as she only wanted to impress him as an intellect, herself took the initiative. She told him that the German State had had no art, science or literature since the war of 1870. She herself only read French or Scandinavian books, and the young German writers, who were just beginning to flourish, had got their inspiration from the North.

But the literature that she called modern was now outmoded in the North, and he found it excruciating to hear her greeting as new, and capable of bearing fruit, ideas that had so recently been abandoned. He did not feel inclined to disown himself and his views, so let the matter pass and suffered in silence. She finally embarked on the "Woman Question" and he, feeling his tail-coat beginning to burst at the seams, looked for the door to the hall and made himself so unbearable that the conversation rapidly dropped off to sleep. When a friend he met on the stairs asked him who the lady was who had interested him for so long, he replied that she was one of those "emancipated" females.

By lying and ruminating over his experiences in this way he reconstructed them in a literary form and thus engraved or riveted them on his mind, so that they were available for future use as surely as savings deposited in a bank. But it was a painful operation, carried out with a feeling of deadly anxiety, and when it was over he fell into a state of unconsciousness resembling sleep, but which was not sleep. He himself called it being "extinguished".

When he awoke, Ilmarinen³ was standing by his bedside. He was the young friend who managed his business with publishers, translators, and theatre managers for him.

"You've not forgotten, have you," he said, "that you've been invited to your Manager's this evening?"

"No, I've not forgotten, but I've told them I can't come."

"If you've done that you're lost. Your play won't be performed."

"It won't be in any case. I've waited in vain now for three months."

"That means it's all the nearer to being performed. He's accepted it and wants to produce it. This is suicide!"

"Certainly! And why not? Do you think I find life so amusing?"

"Give me one good reason why you should hurt his feelings by absenting yourself when the party was arranged partly for you."

"I haven't got a reason. The thing has seized hold of me like an *idée fixe*, a whim, an impulse. I know quite well that I shall lose by it, but I can't do otherwise. At one moment I'm assailed by pangs of conscience, chiefly because I know I shall hurt his feelings, but at the next moment I'm filled with delight, with malicious delight, because I've brought suffering upon myself . . . suffering which I should all the same prefer to avoid."

"You're a strange man, but you've no right to lament your fate, since you yourself stand in your own way."

"Perhaps! But that's how things are, and I can't change myself. Moreover, life has taught me that when I act instinctively, however crazy my behaviour may seem, things turn out all right in the end. If I reason the matter out, or weigh up the pros and cons as they affect me, things go wrong."

"Fatalist! Mind what you're about!"

"No need. I've a feeling that I'm going exactly where I'm allowed to go, and am only doing what I'm intended to do."

"You'll no doubt find out."

"In this particular instance: if the Manager wants my play he'll produce it, even if I fail to go to his party."

"No, he won't, you know. Where are you going this evening?"

"To the Cloister! What day is it today?"

"It's New Year's Eve!"

"Ugh! So we're at the end of this horrible year! I've no doubt there'll be more of them. I'm ready for anything now, for the worst!"

"We'll meet at the Cloister then!"

Snow had really fallen, but wet snow in which wheels cut dark lines, which made the snow look even whiter and the mud blacker. The city was like a corpse in its winding sheet, the air was raw and penetrating, the sky had a sickly hue. It was the sort of day when it was pleasant to creep into the Cloister, for its colourful stained-glass windows always made the weather appear fine.

When you entered the vestibule by the big portico you were greeted by coloured travel-posters, with views of Nice, the

Alps, Heligoland, Dieppe, the Tyrol, Frognesaetern and many other places. These views instantly dilated: the sea was blue, the palms swayed in the southern breeze, the snow of the Alps and the vineyards of the Lake of Geneva made you forget how far north you were and where you lived.

Once properly inside you found yourself in a church-like hall with a vaulted roof and large Gothic windows filled with stained glass. The walls were decorated with pagan scenes in praise of wine, friendship and love, and furnished with mottos in the same spirit. You could then find yourself a table to the left, or to the right, or straight ahead, and select a place of refuge along the winding alleys according to your mood or the company you were in.

Immediately on the right was the counter and the shelves, built inside the hall like a tabernacle or a baptistery, with one gilded column in the Jesuit style, and in the background the door and the steps leading down to the cellar where the ever-lasting lamp burned. Above the tabernacle were the simple but impressive words: *Hier Giebt's Alles!** One could hardly ask for more, and a glance at the shelves did indeed reveal all the delights of this world in bottles, flagons, and casks.

If you continued to the right the place opened out into a chapel with a large table reserved for actors. The arcading was hung with banners and objects reminiscent of the theatre, and the walls decorated with laurel wreaths, portraits of famous actors, diplomas, and advertisements. Small cupboards placed in the corners contained all the requisites for celebrating orgies; miniature fireworks, coloured lanterns, conjurers' outfits, masks, false noses, and so on.

To the left of this pagoda was the Knights' Hall, in which armour and weapons clothed the white-washed walls. The piano was here, also long black tables and benches which provided seats for large numbers of people on great occasions.

* We have everything.

On the left, starting on a level with the counter, was a row of cells, shut in by partitions of sawn oak, in which choir-stalls made pleasant resting-places. Round the counter were two halls and straight ahead a private room that was always booked. In a word, by means of an optical illusion the premises gave the impression of being a never-ending labyrinth, in which you lost your way because you confused right and left.

The place really had everything. Food and drink, a telephone, messengers to run errands in the town, writing materials, so that many people conducted all their business, including authorship, from it. Only actors, artists and literary people patronized it, and all were more or less acquainted with each other. If you were one of the brotherhood you felt at home, and if some inquisitive stranger appeared on the scene he either did not like it, or felt he was intruding on a closed circle. As I said, the place had everything except a clock, which meant that you forgot about time, but that did not matter for they never turned you out, even after cock-crow. Furthermore, most people's object in going there was to forget time, that of the present, and above all that of the past.

It was here, during the last decade of the century, that the Scandinavian emigrants had taken up their abode; an unusual body of talent, seeking recognition, understanding and daily bread; dissatisfied and at loggerheads with the people at home. One of them was as much as fifty, others were round about forty, the age when you first become able to view life in perspective. Some of them were thirty, and resting for a while on newly-won laurels. One of them was still only in his twenties and acted as a famulus.

Worthy of note, and also characteristic of the period, was the fact that four men of our circle had been divorced after having married women who, in some cases, had also been divorced. To find out why the most remarkable of the Scandinavian men of the seventies and eighties chose their wives from among women who were already married would probably be as difficult as reading the book of Fate. It could hardly have been due to any lack of moral fibre, since venturing upon such a terrible operation as a divorce requires a love that is true, pure, and strong, and since it is also ignominious to have to go through life introducing another man's woman as your own. It may be that the young girl, the child, is not the companion an intelligent man is looking for when he sets out to find his woman, his friend, his partner; but that the wife, informed and aware, corresponds better to the image he has formed of a mate who will be his second self. Among these people you saw men deserting beautiful young wives, and going off with ugly, older women, who already had several children. So passion was not at the bottom of it, but instead a disinterested, non-sensual understanding of the purest description, and if you ask: why then did they marry? I answer: because they desired to live together and never to be separated.

The Scandinavians had been joined by a number of natives and a Russian, all of them attracted towards the northern light like moths in search of warmth, but all finding only icy cold. The fact was that towards the end of the era scepticism had crept into the movement, and its members were in process of purging themselves of their naturalistic leaven. The strangers therefore only found faeces where they had come to obtain nourishment. Everyone was on the watch to see who could be the first to find a new formula for the artistic and literary works of the future.

They had talked themselves and each other to a standstill. All subjects of discussion were drained dry and no one believed what anyone else said, since scepticism was the watchword. All the blasphemies and curses they could think of had been hurled at existence, since they no longer saw a chance of penetrating more deeply into the riddle of the universe by means of physiology. All hope of rational conversation was finally abandoned

and they went on meeting only in order to avoid being alone,
and to drink themselves to the point of a night's sleep.

New Year's Eve had brought the Goths together in unusual
numbers, and when Ilmarinen and his older friend entered the
Knights' Hall at the Cloister the party was already in full swing.
The Russian,[4] annoyed because they had refused him a bottle of
cognac, had ordered ten glasses of it which were standing in
front of him on a tray, labelled with the metal disk normally
used for reserving a table, which bore the single word: Private!
This meant that he intended to drink them all himself. "The
Savage",[5] the German poet, had in front of him a glass a foot
tall filled with red wine. He was sitting leaning over his rapier,
the great duelling scars on his face as bright red as dogs'
tongues.

The remaining guests had each ordered whatever they liked
best.

An oppressive silence enveloped the company, and anyone
who dared to throw out a question or a conjecture was immediately cut short with: "What's that you're lying about now?"
Only the Savage, in an ecstasy of poetic frenzy, could be heard
now and then groaning out his final words on all vital questions: "*Kinder erklärt mir das Räthsel der Welt!*"* after which he
would pour down his throat as much wine as could run down
it at one go without choking him. The atmosphere was so
overcharged that some kind of outlet was essential, and this was
provided by the Russian's sitting down to the piano.

He improvised on well-known themes, but only in the grand
manner, and his control over his listeners was so complete that
resistance was impossible. It ceased to be music, and the piano
was forgotten. It was a gale, a waterfall, a thunderstorm, which
turned souls inside out and gathered up whatever was left that
was positive and fertilizing. By the way in which he blended
the themes the whole performance became a splendid concert,

* "Explain the riddle of the universe to me, my children."

to which the voices of Beethoven, Mozart, Wagner, and Chopin each contributed a part. When he had finished applause broke out from other parts of the Cloister. The clatter of it found its way under the vault from the most distant nooks and corners.

New life was put into the tired hordes of the Goths. New ideas were born collectively, so that it was hard to say who had brought them into the world.

The doctor, our medical man, who did not usually practise the literary arts, turned poet and improvised sonorous verses which he sang to the tune of new melodies.

Our Savage recited from his published poems, and speeches followed one upon the other.

The table was covered with bottles, glasses, and plates. Wits sparkled and blossomed. It was a joy to be alive.

"This is how life should always be!" said the Russian, who had grown sentimental at the thought of the dark, poverty-stricken room in the working-class district, where his helpmate and his children were waiting for him.

"I once heard one of a group say the same thing in the same words, and the following day the group was dissolved and its members were deadly enemies," said the Swede, whom we first met in his bed on the morning of that very day.

"Do you believe," said the Russian springing to his feet, "that you and I could ever be enemies?"

"You are born enemies!" cried the Savage, "and the Swede's a demon!"

By way of protest the Russian seized his friend's hand, kissed it, and said with tears in his voice:

"No, you're my father, for you've taught me all I know!"

The Swede, who cherished a genuine and warm feeling of friendship for the gifted man, could not find any corresponding expressions for what he felt, but became cold and reserved, which only inflamed his friend the more. In the simple manner of his native land he took out his door-key and, handing it to his "father", said, so that all could hear:

"You must go to my home, you must sleep with my Maschka, you and no other, for she's always pleased to see you, and you'll be doing me an honour."

This was the Russian's usual way of expressing his friendship, and no one took it to mean more than it did. But in order not to hurt a man who was willing to give another what he himself loved most, you had to accept the key, though this did not necessitate making any movement to go.

The hours passed uncounted, senses were inflamed, wells of memory overflowed. They had so much to tell that they thought they had forgotten and, when two memories met in something observed in common, sympathy blossomed and flourished.

"Why must one suffer such horrible pangs of conscience the next day," asked the Russian, "when one has done no wrong, only gained experience, added to the store of one's ideas, known the illusion of loving others and being loved oneself?"

"Yes, why indeed? Socrates would have blamed the jealous gods, who begrudge mankind all joy."

The hum of voices in the alleys of the Cloister had long been audible. Now, from the actors' chapel, came the sound of singing, led by guitars and mandolins. The serious part was over, and the orgy began, first hesitantly, as when children are at play, but later the beast was let loose and demons flapped their batlike wings.

First armour and weapons were taken down from the walls. Clad in cuirasses and with lances in their hands the Savage and the Dane engaged in a jousting bout that could have ended badly. After that the battle of Fehrbellin was enacted, in which the Scandinavians, contrary to the evidence of history, held the field.

They now heard the rattle of revolver shots coming from the

actors' chapel, and when they hastened thither, they were greeted by a little display of fireworks, let off from the actors' private table.

People had now smelt gunpowder and were ripe for anything. The Savage proposed in all seriousness that they should execute the prisoners and set fire to their camp, but at that moment every single person in the Cloister struck up Tararaboom-deré, that infernal tune, which has been able to conquer the whole civilized world merely by knocking on the door of that home for idiots that everyone has at times in the recesses of his everyday soul.

But the Russian's musical instinct rose to the occasion, and when he interrupted this hymn to the banal with a bubbling czardas on the piano, everyone in the Knight's Hall broke into a wild dance. Strains from times immemorial awakened evil passions, reverberations from the sacrificial songs and magic chants of pagan days evoked the primeval man and, in an absolute frenzy, the Savage leapt on the table and continued the dance among the glasses and bottles which he crushed underfoot, and those that his foot could not reach he broke with his sword.

Then, from the alleys of the Cloister, came the sound of the nightwatchman's "Happy New Year". Tankards were clanked, "Estis-ne praeparati?"* yelled the landlord. "Sumus!"† answered the choir, upon which there was drinking and clanking and shouting and embracing, and the whole building resounded with: "Happy New Year!"

"This'll be a lovely New Year, this will!" said the Swede to the Russian.

"Don't speak ill of this year, you, of all people, who can expect only good of it."

"I?"

At that moment he noticed in the distance someone who was

* Are you prepared?   † We are.

regarding him with sullen eyes. It was the actor who should have had the leading part in the play that had been accepted. Their eyes met and they approached each other.

"So you're here, instead of with the Manager!" exclaimed the actor.

"Yes, as you see!"

"You've done yourself no good."

"I realize that. What did he say?"

"He said: 'He shouldn't have done this.' You hurt him deeply, for you failed your lady, Miss X, the actress, who was the cause of your success a year ago. Verses had been printed with which to salute you. It's a great pity."

The Swede took the Russian by the arm and together they walked out into the winter night.

2

Aufschwung

(Soaring: see p. 158)

ON THE 2ND OF JANUARY Ilmarinen and the Swede were walking past the Lessing theatre when two ladies, both very well dressed, hurried by. The Finn raised his hat to them.

"Why didn't you greet them?" he asked the Swede.

"I didn't know either of them. Who were they?"

"One was the lady with whom you had such an animated conversation at that dinner party the other day."

"Was it she? I really didn't notice what she looked like. You could introduce me to her all over again, and I should never know you were introducing me to an acquaintance."

They then steered a course to the Cloister, where they met all the members of their circle, today enlarged by some lady artists. It was high time for the company to be enlivened by a new element, especially of the female sex, for topics of conversation had been worn threadbare, and the general tone had become coarse and acrimonious. Now everyone was competing in their efforts to appear at their best.

Then someone discovered that the Danish painter[6] had been absent for several days, and in response to enquiries, one of the ladies volunteered the information that someone had come to Berlin to see him.

"A lady, I suppose, since he does not dare to bring his guest here?"

"Yes, a lady, she's a painter."[7]

The conversation wound in and out. Many of those present, who were in the habit of using simple, straightforward words, had to hunt for synonyms more suitable for the ears of ladies.

Meanwhile Ilmarinen had got hold of an evening paper, but he suddenly broke off his reading of it and turned to the Swede:

"Just look at this! Look! Your play is being rehearsed and is going to be performed in two weeks' time."

"If that's true it doesn't make sense! But that's how it's always been for me. Whenever I've done something stupid I've succeeded, while anything I've shown forethought about, or weighed up, has come to nothing. Isn't it strange? So strange that I long ago gave up believing that I've the least influence over my own fate."

"Yes, indeed, you're an odd man and everything in your life seems to work backwards."

The Savage arrived and could not conceal his disgust at the introduction of ladies.

"I've females enough at home"—he was in fact married—"and I come here to be coarse. I don't like this at all. I don't enjoy company in which I mustn't say s—t!"

They then began to sing some inoffensive patriotic songs in chorus, the ladies joining in, and the Savage announced that the atmosphere was stuffy.

After this the Dane arrived, but alone. He was assailed by impertinent questions, in particular as to why he had not brought his lady friend with him.

"She's so shy. . . ."

"That's rich! She was out with you at Hopfenblüthen yesterday evening."

The Dane then admitted to the Swede that his friend was very eager to make his acquaintance, but that she was timid about large gatherings, as she came of a very good family.

When his listener pulled a face at this, the Dane immediately made a clean breast of his secret:

"It's true, I'm afraid of you, and I've a feeling that if you two meet something will catch fire."

"Oddly enough I've heard the same words before, on a similar occasion."

"And did something catch fire?"

"Yes."

"Then it would be better if you didn't meet."

"No one escapes their fate, but do as you please."

"What are you whispering about over there?" asked the
Norwegian, who thought he had got wind of an intrigue
which he was not being allowed to share.

"Oh, this Swede is so wise, there isn't anything he hasn't
experienced already. You can't tell him anything new."

"A man of forty knows everything! Life works in such a
simple way, everything is repeated, everything happens again
and again. If you've a couple of rules-of-thumb you can solve
all your problems. That's why life becomes so unbearable after
forty. As far as I'm concerned the family club* might just as
well be reintroduced."

Fourteen days later the play [*Creditors*] was put on successfully, for it was performed seventy-five times without a break.
After the performance there was a dinner at the Rathauskeller,
at which actors, reporters, and literary men were present and
the author sat on the Manager's left. The whole passed off in an
atmosphere of harmony and satisfaction.

Not until they reached the dessert did the Manager turn to
the author and say:

"You didn't come to my party!"

"No, and I shall never be able to tell you my motive for not
doing so."

"Why is that?"

"Because there wasn't one."

But afterwards, and for a long time after that, when he was
sitting with one or other of his friends, he asked himself and
them how it had come about that his play had been performed.
No one could give him an answer, he least of all, for he had

* A club with which useless old people are said to have been killed. One
can be seen in Nordiska Museum, Stockholm.

been told that at the collation, which had taken place a month
before he had been invited to the party, the Manager had
banged together the acting-copy with the words:

"That's a play I shall never produce."

This trifling incident gave the author grounds for believing
that someone was manipulating his destiny, and that what was
intended to happen did happen, even if the invisible threads
could not be detected.

Meanwhile he was on top. How many times had he not been
so before, only to crash to the bottom again. His whole life had
been like a series of tests which never came to an end, and in
which one failure could annul all previous successes. So, while
he had no confidence that all would go smoothly in future, he
went about in a state of quiet satisfaction, undisturbed by any
envy on the part of his friends. They were honestly glad that
at least one of their number had vindicated himself, and in the
glow of his success they read a promise of their own.

There was spring in the air even in February. The Cloister
was still their meeting place, but the Danish painter, who often
absented himself, obstinately refused to bring his lady friend
with him. Nevertheless, most of the others had already caught
a glimpse of her in the street.

"It's you I'm frightened of," he would amuse himself by
saying to the Swede.

"Why so? I'm no Don Juan, and as far as that goes, I've no
right to look at a woman until I've cleared up the matter of my
broken marriage and the obligations connected with it."

"All the same, I'm afraid of you. She's read your books and
never talks of anything but you."

"Don't bring her here then, if you think she might be a
danger to my peace of mind."

His wish was granted, for she did not come.

The author's theatrical success began to be expressed in terms

of invitations, and one evening he went to visit a very important literary man, at whose house the newly-risen stars of the
literary and artistic world were wont to meet. The supper was
long and brilliant, but some seats were unoccupied, as a number
of guests were expected after the theatres closed. At half-past
ten there was a stir at the table, and the expected guests made
their appearance. These were three ladies and two gentlemen,
all unknown to the Swede. But one of the three ladies nodded,
as if she knew him, and held out her hand. He immediately
asked his hostess in a whisper who she was.

"Who! Why, Miss X to whom you talked at Doctor E's
supper party."

"Really? How odd that I, who have such a good memory,
should be quite unable to remember what Miss X looks like.
The other evening I walked past her in the brilliantly-lit foyer
of a theatre, and omitted to bow."

"Indeed! I suppose that, as a woman-hater, you are naturally
unable to see that she is beautiful!"

"Is she?" he said, leaning forward to get a better look at the
young lady, who had sat down at the far end of the table. "Yes,
she's not bad looking!"

"For shame! She's a well-known beauty of the most beautiful Viennese type."

"Is she indeed! It's true that I used to fall in love with nothing
but blondes, but for the last few years my heart has been given
only to dark women."

Whereupon their conversation touched lightly upon other
matters. After supper the party assembled in the drawing-room
and very soon these two, the beautiful Viennese and the
woman-hater, were so deep in conversation that a group of
ladies and gentlemen, smiling mischievously, gathered round
them to watch. But they noticed nothing, only talked and
talked, until their hostess interrupted them by offering them
some tea.

When at last the party broke up, he and she inexplicably
found themselves again in each other's vicinity, so that it was
he who helped her on with her coat. And when she asked who
was going to see her home, he answered: "I am, of course,"
and was accepted.

When they reached the bottom of the stairs they heard the
words: "Good night," followed by a peal of laughter. It was
their charming young hostess, who was leaning over the
bannister.

They walked along Schönenberger-Ufer and past Lützow
Bridge, talking all the time, and by the time they had reached
Courbière-strasse he had been invited to supper with her the
following evening to meet a beautiful young woman artist.
But she warned him that the entertainment in her room would
be very simple, as she lived in a boarding-house kept by a very
strict old lady.

When they parted it was like old friends and colleagues.

He began to stroll homewards in the dark, trying as he went
to reconstruct the events of the evening. He noticed once again
that he was unable to recall what "she" looked like, and he
could not understand this since, as a one-time reporter, he was
used to photographing by eye people, scenes, landscapes, and
interiors. Besides, he had noticed that on this evening, she had
not been at all the same person as on their first encounter. There
had not been a trace of "emancipated" woman about her, only
gentle submissiveness, a hint of melancholy, which suited her
and roused compassion. And when they had talked about anyone in misfortune tears had come into her voice. It was her
voice he remembered, a rather deep and sorrowful voice, with
little inflections that drew one far away from a great city, and
awakened memories of forests and lakes, of the sounds of
nature, of Gainsborough hats and hay rakes. He now remembered how, that evening, people had treated her as a child,

teased her about her writing, begged for her protection, to all of which she had merely smiled. She had even had the misfortune to let fall a number of naïve remarks, which she had originally meant to be taken seriously, though in the course of saying them she had managed to shrug them off.

The only person who had taken her seriously was he, the stranger, the "woman-hater", as he was rightly and wrongly called. For he had seen that this was no child, but a woman, to whom he could talk about all the things that interested him, about people and books, without ever having to annotate what he said.

When he woke the next morning he tried, refreshed as he was, to reconstruct the people and events of the previous day. It was his habit when he made a new acquaintance, to search his memory for their opposite number, as he put it, in order to come to grips with their character. This he did by going through in his mind the friends he already knew well, to find one who resembled the person for whose equation he was seeking. Often enough this psychic operation happened of itself, so that as he was trying to recall the new person, the image of some old friend would emerge and more or less cover the new one. Thus, as he now tried to imagine the Miss X of yesterday, he saw not her, but his own elder sister, a fairly short, dark, female type. As a result, anything of an erotic nature—if such there had been—was eliminated, and his only memory was of a good female friend. It was therefore in a state of complete calm that he presented himself that evening, untroubled by any hint of the concern a man experiences when he sets out to make himself agreeable to a young lady.

For the same reason he was received quite frankly, like an old acquaintance, and found himself in an elegantly-furnished room, with a richly appointed writing-desk, living plants, family portraits, rugs, and comfortable chairs.

As the lady painter had been prevented from coming he had
to put up with only his hostess for company, an arrangement
which seemed to him to conflict somewhat with the conven-
tions. But the young lady's straightforward and unaffected
manner suppressed his desire to comment in a way which
might have caused pain.

So there they sat, opposite to each other, and conversed. She
was wearing a dress of black silk, interwoven with blue threads,
in the empire style, with black lace that fell from her shoulders
like a sleigh-net.* This gave her rather the appearance of a
married woman and, combined with the worldly and experienced tone of her conversation, made him think: "This is a
divorcée!" Her face, which he was now able to examine in full
light, had a forehead so unlined that it looked as if it had been
moulded, which indicated a strong but not obstinate will. Her
eyes were large and well-shaped, like those of the children of
the south, and her nose seemed to have changed its mind as it
grew up, for it took a sudden turn in the middle, and in a trice
became Roman. This unexpected little bit of levity on its part
gave charm to a profile which reminded him of a cameo.

Their conversation went even better this evening, for they
already had a little corpus of mutual experiences to examine,
of acquaintances to analyse, of suggestions to test. They sat
snipping silhouettes of their friends, and as neither wanted to
appear spiteful, they snipped prettily, and not with pointed
scissors.

During this innocent interchange of opinions a very large
flower-basket of glorious roses caught his eye. His hostess
instantly read his thoughts and, just as a servant entered with
wine and cigarettes, she rose and went up to the flowers.

"A friend gave me these when he left," she said.

"She's engaged," he thought, and felt himself superfluous.

* A long net hung over the horse's rump to prevent lumps of frozen snow
from hitting the passengers.

To show him that she was not engaged she roughly broke off a spray, but as this was attached by a metal thread she had to look for some scissors. These were in a needle-work box on the bottom shelf of the whatnot, so she had to go down on her knees and remain kneeling. She was still in this position when she fastened the two most beautiful roses in his buttonhole, and all she had to do in order to drink his health was to stretch out her hand for a glass of wine.

"Roses and wine! I once used them as the refrain of a ballad," he said, finding the situation somewhat bizarre, though in itself insignificant.

"Please recite that ballad for me in your beautiful language!"
He had forgotten it!

She rose and went back to her chair, and he persuaded her to tell him about her life. She had left home early, she told him. Her parents lived apart, but were not divorced as they were Catholics. She had been brought up in convent schools in London, Paris, Italy, and elsewhere, and especially in Paris, with the "English Ladies", she had been tormented by religion, so much so that in the end she had thrown it all overboard. It was true that she was sometimes aware of a vacuum, but like everyone else she was expecting something new to come into the world. For the time being she, like her contemporaries, was chiefly interested in raising humanity out of poverty and freeing it from oppression. She had taken a superficial interest in Nietzsche—like the rest—and put him aside, but not until he had modified her exaggerated hopes of seeing universal equality.

While she was talking he noticed a light shining through a curtain behind her back, screening a door that no doubt led to the flat. The idea that he was the object of a practical joke struck him like a flash of lightning. Perhaps he, the woman-hater, was to be surprised in the ridiculous posture of a wooer? Or was it simply that contact with the flat was being maintained for reasons of decorum? This healthy state of uncertainty

kept the conversation free of flirtatiousness, and when supper
was brought in he blamed himself for having suspected his
kind hostess of evil designs or lack of trust.

At half-past eight he tried to leave, but she only had to
suggest that he was longing for the Cloister to make him stay.

He again tried to go at half-past ten, but was again detained.

"But listen, it's my duty as an older and more sensible person
to avoid putting you in an embarrassing position."

She refused to understand him, explained that she was
independent, and that her landlady was accustomed to her
supper-parties.

Finally his instinct warned him that this was all wrong, and
he rose and took his leave.

As he strolled home he said to himself:

"No, people aren't as simple as all that. You can't solve the
riddle of them with any formulas, and about this evening and
this woman I don't understand a thing!"

They met next time at the New Museum. In her outdoor
clothes she looked like a young married woman of about thirty
or more. There was a tired expression about her mouth, and
tiny, fine lines, like those that people get who are always laughing. But she was depressed, hinted at a rupture with her father,
and a journey she would probably have to make in the near
future. She went on to enquire about her friend's relations with
theatres and publishers, and asked if she could not be of assistance by giving advice and introductions. She was pure
motherly tenderness, while a certain carelessness in her dress
seemed to indicate that she did not wish to please as a woman.

However, when she suggested that they should go to the
theatre together, he refused, for his feelings told him that she
ought not to be compromised, and that he too ought not to
run risks. His economic position was too insecure to withstand
the suspicion that he was having a love affair.

She then proposed that they should go out on the spree together. With this in view he was told to call for her, but at her new address. She had moved, it seemed.

"Aha, turned out of her boarding-house because of me," he thought, but refrained from saying so.

His curiosity as a writer was now aroused, and he wanted to solve the riddle of this woman, for he had never before met anyone capable of changing their shape as she could hers.

When he rang the bell of her lodging that evening he was asked to wait in a drawing-room, and when the young lady was ready he was shown into the hall. The regime here was obviously a different one.

They walked westwards, along a deserted boulevard which led in the direction of the Zoological Gardens, and entered a small restaurant which she seemed to know well. In her fur coat and with a scarf over her head she had looked in the dark like an old woman, and when she bent forward slightly as she walked it made him think there was something witch-like about her. But when they entered the brightly lit premises, and she took off her fur and her scarf, she was suddenly transformed into a youthful beauty. A simple, close-fitting, moss-green dress revealed the figure of an eighteen-year-old, and her hair, which she wore brushed back, made her look like a grown-up school-girl. He could not conceal the effect this magic had on him, but let his eyes sweep over her whole person, as if he were seeking for some hidden enemy with a searchlight.

"Eros! Now I'm lost!" he thought, and from that moment he was.

She very well saw the effect she had produced and she phos-phoresced, sat as if enveloped in light, sure of victory, her expression triumphant, for she saw that the woman-hater was conquered.

Fright took hold of him. She had his soul in the pocket of her dress; she could fling it into the river, or the gutter, and this

added hatred to his feelings for her. He saw his only hope of
salvation in the influence his flame might have in kindling hers,
so that she became as surely bound to him as he was to her.
With this half-formed aim in view he did what any man in his
position would have done; he crept close to her, made himself
as small as a child, roused her compassion, but the noble compassion of a merciful being towards a broken human soul, a
soul condemned, that saw no hope of bliss. She listened and
received what he gave as a tribute, listened calmly, majestically,
maternally, but not spitefully like a coquette.

When, after a cold supper, they began to think of leaving, he
rose to look up a train in a time-table. On returning to the table,
meaning to pay the bill, he was told by the waiter that it had
already been settled. Who had paid? The young lady!

At this he flared up and, wrongly suspecting that she believed
he had no money, he insisted that at least he should be allowed
to pay for himself.

"I don't know the customs of your country," he exclaimed,
"but here in Berlin and in my country, it's a disgrace for a man
to let a lady pay for him."

"You were my guest!"

"No, we went out together. We shall never be able to come
here again. Don't you understand the sort of reputation you've
got me? Don't you realize the horrible name this waiter may
call me?"

And when the waiter was summoned so that the matter
could be rearranged, a new scene developed, which made him
rise in anger, and put his share of the bill on the table.

She was upset, but would not admit that she had done anything wrong.

Discord prevailed. He saw now that she was what is called
"thoughtless", thoughtless in the way she had been when she
invited him by himself to her room so late in the evening. Or
was it her way of expressing the emancipated woman's demand

that she should be treated as man's equal in everything? A
flying in the face of convention and supposed prejudices?
Perhaps the latter, but he felt that he was being bullied, and he
was angry.

Out in the street the silence between them was beginning to
be unpleasant when she held out her hand, and said in her
warm, sincere voice:

"Don't be cross!"

"No, I won't, but, but . . . never do that again."

They parted friends and he hastened away to the Cloister.
He had not been there for a long time, partly because of a
certain feeling of repugnance for the tone of the place, which
was not in harmony with his mood, and partly because he had
promised his new friends that he would be abstemious.

He found the company as before, but felt something of a
stranger, and knew very definitely that he would never bring
her there. For this reason he soon went home and became lost
in meditations, which sometimes took on a dark hue and sometimes a brighter one. But when his thoughts turned back to the
moment when her youthful loveliness had crept out from the
animal skin of her fur, it seemed to him to have something
horrible, something ominous about it. What he had seen was
not the virgin loveliness that mirrors the paradise of childhood,
but the dark, diabolical beauty that is death to men, the grave
of their will-power, that brings humiliation, ruin, infamy, and
haggling, but which is as unavoidable and as inescapable as
fate.

The next day he was invited to go with her to a dinner-party
at the house of a Professor of Art.

On this occasion she had assumed a new guise: a supercilious
woman of the world, conversing in an assured tone of voice,
uttering successful witticisms, epigrams, and never at a loss if
anyone riposted. At times she was nonchalant, blasé, cruel.

The Professor, who had just returned from sitting on a jury, told them that he had helped to sentence a woman who had murdered her child.

"I should have acquitted her," interposed Miss X.

The Professor, who was a member of the Academy, and the portrait painter and intimate of the Kaiser's, was thunderstruck, but did not reprove her. He took her remark as a caprice and dropped the subject.

The atmosphere was rather oppressive in other ways too, and the stranger, who had been invited by the lady of the house, felt himself to be an unsuitable guest in a house where everything revolved round the Kaiser and the Court. In all probability his friend had contrived this invitation with the kindly intention of making him known, and of helping a man who had the reputation of being half an anarchist to acquire a veneer of man of the world. The disharmony soon became apparent when the conversation turned to art, and the Professor proved to be alone in his views and his academic ideals.

While dessert was being served his hostess asked him if he would not come to their evening "At Home", where he would meet many famous people. For this she received such a sharp look from her husband that the stranger, who had observed the look, thanked her, but made up his mind not to accept the invitation. The fact was that Scandinavians in particular were out of favour in high circles, because a Norwegian painter's new-fangled style of painting had caused a rupture in the Academy.

Once again he had let himself be made a fool of by his friend's thoughtlessness in introducing him into a circle where he could not feel at home, and where he was not welcome. She herself did not appear to notice that anything was wrong, but seemed just as much at home and just as carefree as before.

After dinner there was music, and the young beauty behaved as if her friend did not exist. She never looked at him, and

when the party broke up, she said goodbye as if she were speaking to a stranger, and let another gentleman see her home.

It was on a Sunday afternoon in February. They were taking
a walk in the Zoological Gardens and the outer boulevards of
the western part of the city, where they were sure of not meeting acquaintances. Finally they entered a secluded café.

She talked of the journey she was about to make, and he
confessed that he would miss her companionship.

"Come too," she said, simply and impulsively.

"Why not? It doesn't really matter to me where I am."

The idea seemed to disperse some clouds, and she then began
to describe Munich, discussed the theatrical prospects there, and
other matters of the same nature.

"But," he objected. "I should be such a long way from my
children."

"Your children, yes, of course; I've so often thought of them.
Haven't you any pictures of them? Do please let me see them."

He really had some photographs with him, and when she
repeated her request, he handed them to her. She showed little
interest in the girls but when she saw the fair-haired, eight-year-
old boy, gazing upwards with his glorious eyes, she fell into
an ecstasy.

"What a lovely face he has! Isn't it a happiness to possess
such a child?"

"To possess today, and to lose tomorrow!"

She began to study the picture and to compare the face in it
to the father's. He thought her rather bold, and experienced the
shyness a man feels towards a woman when she appropriates
his role.

"He is you," she said, "and yet not you."

He did not ask her to explain and she begged him to let her
keep the picture by her.

Their conversation continued and returned to the subject of

her journey, but her attention wandered and her eyes frequently
rested on the photograph.

He could not guess what was going on in her soul, but he
could see that a struggle was taking place, and that she was on
the point of reaching a decision. He became aware too that
many fibrous roots were worming their way from her being
and entwining themselves in his. Something fateful was happening. He felt oppressed. He longed for the circle of male friends
that he had abandoned, and begged her to release him from his
promise not to visit the Cloister.

"Are you longing to get back to that *pit*?" she said, in her
maternal voice. "Think of your little son."

They left the café and walked silently out into the dark but
starry night. He offered her his arm for the first time, and the
pelerine of his coat, fluttering in the wind, struck her in the
face.

"This happened to me once in a dream," she said.

But he did not answer.

When they reached her door she caught both his hands in
hers, and gazing into his eyes she said:

"Don't go there! Don't go to your friends."

Whereupon she let down her veil and, before he had time to
guess what she was going to do, she pressed a kiss upon his lips,
through her veil. But by the time he stretched out his arms to
embrace her she was inside the door, and it was shut. He stood
there utterly dumbfounded, unable to grasp how it had happened. First came the thought: "she loves me, she hasn't been
playing with me!" Then: "but how bold! True she let down
her veil, that was a sign of modesty, and she fled in astonishment
over her own action. That was original, but not unashamed.
Other countries, other customs!"

But it was rather humiliating for a man to receive the first
token instead of giving it. All the same he would never have
dared to risk getting his ears boxed or being laughed at. . . .

Just as well that it had happened. He knew now where he stood, and that was satisfactory.

She loved him! To be loved was like being able to say to oneself: "I'm not so bad after all since someone can look up to me, can think well of me." And thereupon self-esteem, hope and trust were revived. He felt young again and ready to begin a new spring. It was true that he had only shown her his good sides, but the habit of temporarily suppressing the bad ones had made him search out those that were good. In this lay the secret of the ennobling effects of love. There was no deception about it. By playing the part of a magnanimous character one might quite well enter so completely into the role that it became second nature. Their liking for each other had arisen as a result of mutual regard and friendship, which showed that it was of the right quality. He had only subsequently discovered that she was beautiful, and been fascinated by her as a woman, and this was a further guarantee that things had developed in the proper order, and that he had not merely been dazzled by a lovely exterior. Of course he had guessed her failings and closed his eyes to them, but that was both the duty of a lover and his most severe test, for without leniency there could be no love.

He went home in a cab and wrote the letter that had to be written. Its concluding words were as follows: "Now the woman-hater lays his head in your lap as a sign that the good in you has triumphed over the evil in him. But do not abuse your power, for if you do you must expect the usual fate of the tyrant."

The next morning he sent off the letter by a messenger.

Ilmarinen was standing at the foot of his bed. He wore an air of secrecy.

"Well," he said, "so you're off again!"

"Yes, it looks like it!"

"And you really dare?"

"Dare to be miserable at the worst. I'm miserable as it is."

"Of course, of course!"

"It makes a change, and this solitary life is not life."

Meanwhile, instead of an answer to his letter he got a telegram, proposing that they should meet that evening together with an editor who might be useful.

To this he replied with a telegram saying: "Not coming until I've had an answer to my letter."

Another telegram in reply. She begged to be allowed to postpone giving her answer until the following day.

The whole performance seemed to him senseless, but he went to meet her as she had proposed. She met him as if nothing had happened. They had supper and talked business. The editor was a married man, a genial person, who seemed to have no pretensions to being an admirer.

But on this evening she seemed to him ugly. She was carelessly dressed, her fingers were inky, and her conversation was so business-like that he thought her quite detestable.

He had had many strange experiences in his life, and met many strange people, but he had never before been involved in anything as crazy as this.

He returned home with sensations of relief, firmly determined not to accompany the young lady to Munich, or to allow his fate to become more closely entwined with hers.

On the following day he received her answer in a letter which further strengthened his resolve to withdraw.

She wrote: that she belonged to the type of woman who could not love. ("Whatever kind of creature is that?" he thought. "It sounds to me like a literary invention.") *He* believed that he loved her, but when he was really only in love with his own infatuation . . . ("Alexander Dumas *fils*, I think!") She begged that she might always remain his friend, and proposed another meeting that day.

To this he replied by thanking her and bidding her farewell.

Then came a hail of telegrams and express letters, and towards evening a waiter announced that a lady was waiting outside in a cab.

At first he thought of saying no, but reflected that if he did she would come up to his room, which would simply knot his bonds. He therefore went down, got into the cab, and without reflection or discussion they met in a kiss which seemed entirely natural.

A heated argument followed, which bore a strong resemblance to a quarrel.

She demanded that he should accompany her on her journey that very evening, but this he definitely refused to do since, if they were seen together, all tomorrow's Berlin papers would be full of the "abduction", and this his conscience would not allow, either for the sake of her parents, or for that of his own children. He was still dependent on other people for help, and the moment he got the reputation of being an adventurer, all sources of assistance would dry up.

"You don't love me!"

"Tut, tut, my little one, don't start that again!"

He was forced to laugh at her. They dismounted from the cab and continued the rumpus down a little green lane that led to the river. Now and then he took hold of her neck and silenced her lips with a kiss.

"I've noticed that you're a madcap, but I'm half mad myself, let me tell you, and you won't get anywhere with me."

"I'll throw myself in the river," she cried.

"Good! I'll jump in after you, and I can swim."

Finally he got her to laugh and they went into a café to try to reach a decision.

He now had the upper hand and treated her like a wayward little girl. Curiously enough, he had no sooner assigned this role to her than she accepted it and continued to play it.

Did these people love each other? Yes, certainly, for he knew quite well how attached he had become and she, as later transpired, had already written a letter to her mother in which she had confessed her love, but *he* must not know of it, for if he did she would immediately be "subjugated".

Meanwhile they came to the following decision: she should travel alone; they would not promise each other anything. They would correspond, bide their time, and see if they could not meet in the summer. Later, when his position was more assured, they would think of getting engaged and married.

This settled, they parted, and were not to meet again for a long time.

He immediately directed his steps towards the Cloister. There, among his friends, he would find himself again. During this month-long state of isolation with a woman he had come adrift from his proper setting, lost his footing, built up a relationship on an illusory foundation by basing it on a young girl, whom, in his infatuation, he had metamorphosed into a mature woman. Her last outburst had shown him a fury, who believed she could frighten him into blind submission. During it the expression of her face had continually changed from a Punchinello's broad grin to the grimaces of a hissing cat, showing her white fangs.

He breathed freely, experienced a sensation of relief, and entered the Cloister with the feeling that he had put something troublesome behind him, something that he had happily survived, and that was now over!

The Dane was there and, having probably been misled by the gossip about the Swede's engagement, he had brought his lady with him. She was a tall, disembodied blonde, who seemed to be emaciated by illness. There was woe and despair in her voice. She spoke with a drawl and her eyes drooped.

As an artist, though an unknown one, she was "emancipated"

as it was called, but not from the feminine vanity of always appearing attended by male hangers-on, whom she could boast she had conquered.

The woman-hater had long occupied her thoughts and now, when at last they met, he was new, full of surprises and, in addition, brought with him all the fire of his newly-awakened passion.

Within half-an-hour she was no longer looking at her old friend or listening to what he said, and after she had given him a final snub, he got up to go. When he enquired if she intended to come with him, her answer was: "You can go." And he went.

In less than an hour she had broken with her friend of many years' standing—whose prophecy had thus come true—and she was now allied with the Swede, who only half an hour before had been kissing his bride-to-be goodbye.

It did not cross his mind to wonder how this could be possible, but he did not allow himself time to reflect upon the matter. She had the advantage of being able to understand his own language. He was able to talk to his heart's content after a long period of imprisonment. He only needed to hint at a thing and he was understood. She drank in the torrent of his words, appeared able to follow his prancing thoughts, and most likely got answers to many of the questions that she had been wanting to ask for a long time.

But she was ugly and badly dressed, and there were moments when the idea that he might be taken for her wooer made him feel ashamed. At such moments he felt indescribable compassion for her, but she took this to mean that he was subjugated.

They went out into the city and wandered from café to café, talking all the time. Sometimes his conscience pricked him, and sometimes this woman, who had been faithless to her friend, disgusted him. But faithlessness was the point at which they met, and they both felt that some relentless fate had driven them together, so that both might commit the same crime on the same evening. Right from the beginning she had asked him about his engagement, and at first he had answered evasively. But when she had gone on questioning him with the understanding of a close friend, he had told her the whole story. When he began to talk of his love he grew warm, and she in turn was warmed by his flame, and threw back reflections of "the other". In this way the image of each woman fell on that of the other, and the absent girl, the very person who should have stood as a barrier between them, became the person who drew them together.

The next day they met again, and as before she never tired of returning to the same subject, his fiancée. But now she analysed, interpreted, and began to throw out doubts about his chance of happiness. She went to work cautiously, handled him tactfully, and only tried her hand at a little objective psycho-analysis.

She also knew how to avoid frightening him off by retracting a word that had been too harsh at exactly the right moment.

As bad luck would have it a letter from his beloved arrived at midday. It should have been an answer to his impassioned goodbye-letter, but she only wrote about business matters, gave him good advice in a high-handed manner; in a word, it was pedantic and pettifogging, and showed not a trace of the young girl. This depressed him and inspired such strong feelings of revulsion that, when he again met his new friend, he became possessed by a tremendous destructive urge to analyse the other woman under a microscope. His friend, with her feminine understanding of the secrets of womanhood, was not slow to put the worst interpretation on all the little details he imparted. He had thrown his lamb to a she-wolf, who was now tearing her victim to pieces under his very eyes.

Three weeks later, at the beginning of April, the Swede was

sitting in the Cloister one afternoon with Laïs, as the company now called her, since she had become everyone's friend without being attached to anyone in particular.

The woman-hater, who was as usual prepared for anything, was wearing a resigned expression. His engagement had proved difficult to keep alive by post, and had become even more precarious since rumours had reached the ears of the lady's father, and made the latter quite frantic. He was a Privy Counsellor, frequented the Court, had twelve orders, ran the official newspaper, and would rather have shot himself than become the father-in-law of a known nihilist. In order to rid himself of the nuisance he had dictated his terms, with which of course they could not comply. He had stipulated that all debts must be paid and a reasonable income guaranteed. As it is impossible for a dramatist, who lives by favour of the public, to guarantee anything, the suitor no longer regarded himself as a candidate, and considered himself free, which indeed he was. Moreover, the humiliating correspondence about money had cooled his ardour. Love-letters full of figures, motherly advice, practical instructions about publishers and the like, had not proved elevating reading for a literary freebooter. Consequently the correspondence had languished and was now in a dying condition, and he regarded himself as free to do as he liked. Laïs, with her usual vanity, had ascribed the honour of causing the breach to herself, though she had no reason for doing so. However, during the last few days something had happened which proved very fortunate in view of subsequent developments. An old friend of Laïs's[8] had arrived from the North and, as he was somewhat in love, she was receiving sufficient attention to prevent her from noticing the woman-hater's increasing indifference to her.

In order to celebrate the new arrival the last few days had been one long party, and now everyone was in the strange state of disintegration when the seams of the soul have, as it were, come apart, and let out thoughts indiscriminately and with no consideration for others.

Laïs, who was obsessed by the not unusual idea that she was irresistible, and was eager to let it be understood that all her male friends were discarded lovers, even in cases where she herself had been discarded, now wanted to show her newly-arrived friend how well provided she was. She therefore began to skirmish with the woman-hater.

As the latter had long entertained for her the hatred which springs from having incautiously entrusted confidences, he now seized the opportunity of breaking with her decently in order to avoid becoming an enemy. In other words he wanted to place her in a position in which neither of them would look slighted.

Perhaps prompted partly by a feeling that something was going to happen to him, he made some excuse or other and said goodbye, intending to leave the two of them alone. But Laïs insisted that he should stay, probably in order to give herself the chance of leaving him by himself when she went off with the other man. However, she had miscalculated, and making a gesture of invitation to the stranger, he left after discharging his parting shot:

"I'll leave you two alone now."

When he got out into the street he experienced a feeling of uneasiness, as if he had left behind him something not concluded, and had something unexpected in front of him. It seemed to him that he could still hear the hissing voice of the woman he had just left. The fact was that when she talked she never opened her lips, which were carved like a snake's, but produced the sounds from her throat, which was always husky from late nights, strong drink and tobacco smoke. He called this sort of voice a "porter voice" when it belonged to a woman, because it reminded him of that black "night-cap" and the environments in which it is found.

"That's friendship with women for you! It always ends in love or hate, just like love itself."

When he reached his hotel he was met by the waiter with a local telegram.

"This is what drew me home," he said to himself, for experience had taught him to believe in telepathy. He had such a firm belief in it, that if at a party they wanted to send for some absent friend he would say: "Shall we send for him telepathically?"

Before he opened the telegram he felt he knew what it said, and when he read it, it seemed to him that he had read it before. Its contents therefore did not surprise him. It said: "I'm here. Come to me at Doctor XX's. Important news." And (in bad Swedish): "I love you so much."

He stood still for a few minutes trying to make up his mind what to do. Then he washed, got into bed, and rang for the waiter.

When the latter appeared he asked him to telephone to his friend the doctor, a married man who had his own private clinic, and an unimpeachable reputation.

The doctor came immediately and had the situation explained to him.

"You're not thinking of retreating, are you?"

"No, but I must collect myself and sleep for twelve hours; my nerves are not under control. I'm going to send a telegram to say I'm not well. She won't believe me, but will come to see for herself. I beg you therefore, please wait here for half-an-hour."

The telegram was sent and half-an-hour later they heard steps in the corridor.

She entered. She was dressed in black and to begin with very suspicious. But being able to consult the doctor and join him in giving advice gave her an advantage, and this pleased her.

They arranged that she should come again the following

morning with the doctor, whereupon she departed, but not until she had smuggled a kiss on to the invalid's hand.

"You shouldn't play with your emotions," said the doctor, who had remained behind. "This woman loves you and you love her! That's something you should cherish."

He lay alone for the whole of that long evening trying to bring some order into the medley, but failing. What a tangled thicket was the human soul! Who could disentangle it? From hatred to contempt, over to respect and admiration, and then back again, a leap to one side and then two forwards. Good and evil, sublime and ridiculous, faithlessness and everlasting love simultaneously, kisses and blows, slanderous accusations and boundless admiration.

Knowing the human soul as he did he had set up among his few basic principles the following: never take anything back, never go back yourself, simply go on winding up the ball. And when, in the early days of their friendship she had tried to refer to something he had said on a previous occasion, he had cut her short with: "Don't go back, simply wind on. One talks so much and most of it is pure improvisation. I've no views, only impromptu ideas, and anyhow life would be pretty dull if one were to think and say the same thing every day. Let's have something new. The whole of life is a fantasy, and it's much more fun to float over the morass than to put down your feet to feel for firm ground where none exists."

This must have corresponded very closely to her own conception of life, for she readily accepted her role. Thus they found each other always new, always full of surprises, and could never take each other quite seriously. And when some discussion arose, and one of them came out with an opinion held by the other the previous day which flatly contradicted the one he or she had abandoned, they were obliged to laugh at their own folly.

For this reason they never got to the bottom of each other

and, at moments when they were quite serious, could burst out simultaneously with: "Who are you? What kind of a creature are you really?"—questions which neither of them could answer.

Just as he was falling asleep he thought: "I won't decide anything, for I've never known a decision come to anything. The course of events must steer my destiny as it has always done."

The next day she arrived before the doctor. Her face wore a knowing expression as much as to say that she knew all about that illness of his, but wasn't going to take any notice of trifles. From a basket she had with her she took a birch-rod.

"What's that?"

"Why, it's an Easter birch, of course. It's Good Friday today."

So saying she tucked in the rod at the foot of his bed, and proceed to decorate the whole room with twigs of pussy-willow in bloom.

She busied herself about the room like a little wife, tidied it up and took stock of the result. Finally she sat down in a comfortable chair.

"Well now! What's the great news?"

"That we must get engaged at once. The papers have already announced that we are."

"Have they indeed? And what about your father?"

"He's resigned to the inevitable, but he's not pleased. Well! Aren't you going to congratulate me?"

"You must congratulate me first, for I'm the elder."

"And the more prudent."

"I have much pleasure in congratulating you. What a husband!"

They prattled on, but soon turned to the chapter called "Prospects". He dictated and she wrote. So-and-so many plays accepted for performance. Good for a thousand!

"With a deduction of thirty per cent for miscalculation," she added.

"Thirty! I always allow ninety per cent for miscalculations, sometimes a hundred."

"Be sensible, please, this is serious. . . ."

And then they laughed.

What divine levity! To look down upon the horrible seriousness of life as if it were something you could blow away; to have the poet's carefree way of treating money matters as if they were poetry.

"How could we endure the misery of life if we didn't treat it as unreal? If I were to take it seriously I should sit and weep all day, and I've no desire to do that."

One practical suggestion emerged: she would learn his language and translate his works herself, which would be a great economy. As far as their marriage went, that was a distant prospect, planned for the autumn at the earliest.

His dinner arrived. She laid it on the low table by the divan, fed him, and was particularly sparing with the wine.

"You've drunk enough for the present, and you must promise me never to go to the Cloister again, least of all with Thaïs."

"With Laïs," he corrected her, with a blush. "So you've heard about that too?"

"Wer dreiundzwanzig Jahre alt ist, der weiss Alles!"*

He was so thankful to be spared the misery of a scene of confession that he promised never again to visit the Cloister. He kept his promise too, as it was the only form of penance he could offer for his villainous behaviour.

They were now engaged, and her company became his only social contact. On the other hand she continued to attend family parties, to visit the theatre, and to fulfil the usual

* If you're twenty-three you know everything.

engagements which her profession as a journalist required. In
their eventual struggle for power she therefore had an advantage. She had a social life from which she could draw moral
support and new inspiration, while he was forced to live on
himself and his former experiences. They really lived as play-
fellows, for he was never allowed to read anything she wrote
for the papers, and though she had read everything he had
written, she was not allowed to admit it, and never did either.
There was nothing in their relationship to suggest that he was
the well-known and experienced author, and she the young
literary and theatrical critic. They met as man and woman, for
as they were to be man and wife he had put himself on her level,
not over her.

As he now saw no one but her he sometimes felt imprisoned,
isolated, and in her power. If he were to break with her now he
would be alone in the world, for he had grown away from his
former friends and developed a distaste for café life. He also
began to feel that he had grown to be part of this woman, and
that separated from her he would wilt away. In spite of her love
she could not keep to herself the fact that she had him at her
mercy, and she sometimes let him know it. Then he would
rage like a lion in a cage, would go out and look up his old
friends, regardless of the fact that he was not happy with them,
and that his conscience pricked him as if he had been unfaithful.
She would sulk for half a day and then creep close to him, go
down on her knees, and be forgiven.

"At bottom," he said on one occasion, "we hate each other
because we love each other. We're afraid of losing our indivi-
duality through the assimilating powers of love, and therefore
we have to break out from time to time, in order to feel that *I*
is not *you*."

She agreed that was so, but it did not help when the spirit of
rebellion was abroad, when the self was fighting for its own
rights. She loved him as a woman loves a man, and she thought

him handsome, though in fact he was ugly. Nor was she given
a chance to forget that he was a noted and a famous person. His
bust was being modelled, three different portraits were being
painted, and his successful play was still on the hoardings. He
for his part demanded neither respect nor admiration, only a
reasonable degree of trust and a friendly manner. She was
usually sparklingly merry, playful without being irritating,
adaptable and charming.

When he sometimes reflected on the many different types he
had observed in the early days of their acquaintanceship he
could hardly understand how she had been able to play so
many roles. Of the emancipated literary woman, with Madame
Staël's open mouth and flowing tongue, not a trace remained.
The grand woman of the world, the mournful Sappho, the
fin de siècle lady, with her macabre paradoxes and her coquetries
of the scaffold, had vanished completely. She saw how modest
he was and she became like him.

April came and with it full spring. His prospects brightened
too. Plays were accepted, a novel sold for quite a considerable
sum, and one of his plays was performed in Paris.

A rumour had been spread about that they were living
together, which was not true. But it alarmed her parents and
they urged them to marry at once.

"Do you want to get married now?" she asked.

"Of course I do!"

And so the matter was settled.

But difficulties arose. She was a Catholic, and as such forbidden to marry a divorced man so long as his wife was
alive.

There was one way of avoiding this stumbling block. They
could get married on Heligoland, where an old English law
was still valid, so they made up their minds to do that. Her
sister arrived to act as a witness. She was married to a famous
artist and was herself a writer. She was therefore able to

appreciate talent even when unaccompanied by worldly wealth.

And so they set out upon their wedding-journey.

It was a May morning on the little sea-girt island. He and she had wandered out to the furthest point where the cliffs plunged down steeply into the sea. He wanted to ask her something while they were alone, but he did not dare, and they were therefore standing silently, gazing into the blue void, seeking a goal that was not there.

They had been there for six days without being able to get married. As a result of negligence his divorce certificate had not been issued until two months after the decree was passed, and it was so dated that the qualifying period had not elapsed. Telegrams with the authorities had been exchanged, but muddle and misunderstanding had resulted in postponement, and her sister had grown impatient.

"Do you trust me?" he asked.

"I believe in your honesty, but you are a bird of ill omen."

"And your sister?"

"What is she to think? She doesn't know you, and all she can see is that your assurances that your papers were in order have proved incorrect."

"She's right, but it's not my fault. What's she going to do now?"

"She's going back tomorrow, and I must go with her."

"So we're to be divorced even before we're married. I'm to go back to a hotel room, to the taverns and the night cafés!"

"No, not that!" And then, after a pause: "Let's jump into the sea."

He threw his arms round her.

"Have you ever met such an unfortunate person as I am? Wherever I go I bring bad luck and ruin. What will your parents say?"

"Don't talk like that. If we're patient we shall win through this too."

"Only to get into other trouble!"

"Come here, I'll blow it away."

And she did indeed blow the clouds away. Divine light-heartedness broke through again, and they raced each other home across the fortifications and the mines.

That evening the decisive telegram arrived and the marriage was fixed for the following morning.

It really happened too, first before the Prussian Mayor. When they were exchanging their vows the bride had a fit of hysterical laughter which threatened to reduce the whole per-formance to naught, as her serious husband had no idea what to make of such a lunatic scene. The wedding party that assembled in the parsonage later that evening was not very magnificent either. Besides the bride's sister there were four pilots, brought in to act as witnesses when they pledged their vows of fidelity "before God".

3

Marriage and Running the Gauntlet

FOURTEEN DAYS OF MAY had elapsed. The couple were
sitting outside their cosy cottage watching the birds of
passage resting in the garden before pursuing their way to the
north.

"How peaceful it is!" she said.

"For how long?"

"For another eight days! But I never thought that marriage
would turn out to be such a splendid institution."

"In spite of the fact that people have called me a woman-
hater I've always loved woman, and though they say I'm the
friend of immorality, I've always stood up for marriage."

"Could you contemplate living alone again?"

"No, the very idea stifles me."

"Do you know that I'm so happy that I'm afraid?"

"So am I. I've a feeling that someone is lying in wait for us.
She is called Nemesis, and she does not persecute evil-doers
only, but also happy people."

"What do you fear most?"

"That we should fall out."

"But surely that depends on us?"

"If only that were so! But strife comes from without, with
the wind, with the dew, with too much sunshine, with rain.
Try to discover which of us was to blame for our last squabble."

"Neither of us was!"

"Neither of us. Then there must have been a third person.
Who was this third person? In order to give him a name people
call him Misunderstanding. But there was nothing wrong with
our understanding. We both knew perfectly well what the
other meant."

"Don't try to frighten me!"

"No, but be prepared to see the same thing happen again, and try to realize that we shall blame each other then as we did last time."

"How about going in and writing?" she said suddenly.

"I can't write."

"Nor can I. My father is angry because I haven't sent him an article for two months."

"And I haven't had an idea for a whole year. Where will this lead us?"

The fact was that they seemed to have reached a state in which they neutralized each other, so that neither of them reacted any more, and their life together consisted of nothing but a peaceful and agreeable silence. And so great was their need of being in each other's company, that neither could go out of a door without being followed by the other.

They tried to shut themselves up in their own rooms to work, but after a quarter of an hour there would come a knock on the door.

"D'ye know, this is simply lovely, but I'm turning into an idiot," she would complain.

"You too?"

"You too!"

"I can neither read, think, nor write any more. Why, I can hardly speak."

"It's because we're too happy. We must go out and meet other people, otherwise we shall turn into nitwits."

The truth was that they had ceased to talk to each other. They were so clearly of one mind in all their views and their likes and dislikes, and they understood each other so well, that there was never any need to exchange opinions. The same tastes, the same habits, the same failings, the same lighthearted scepticism had drawn them to each other, and now they were fused together like two pieces of the same metal. They had lost themselves and their individual shapes and they were one. But the memory of an independent being, of a personal existence still survived, and a war of liberation was on the threshold. Their instincts of self-preservation were reawakening, and as they both tried to resume their own personality, you could hear the sound of the pieces being torn apart.

"Why can't you write?" he asked.

"I've tried, but the only result is you and what concerns you."

"Oh well, it comes to much the same thing whether it's me or someone else."

"You mean I've no ideas of my own?"

"You're too young to have any of your own. You're only a reflection of other people, and I'm as good as the next man."

It would have been better if he had left that unsaid, for now she was properly roused.

The silence between them began to make them uneasy and in the midst of a loving embrace each was aware that the other was now sharpening the knife that would sever their bonds.

Then came a newspaper containing an announcement that a play of his, which had long been accepted, was going to be performed in London, and that an English publisher had a volume ready for the press.

"Shall we go to London?" she asked.

"Willingly, though I never believe these announcements. I've read them too often. Still, it might be a business trip that would pay for itself."

They decided to go and were soon on their way. They saw the little red promontory disappear with the same delight they had felt when they first saw it looming out of the mist.

In Hamburg they had to spend a day at an hotel. On returning from a walk he found his wife sealing up six packages all of a similar size and shape.

"What have you got there?" he asked.

"Oh, it's the story of your Italian journey which I'm sending to newspapers I know in Germany."

"But it can't be split up. You know quite well that it's a coherent whole. Have you read it?"

"No, I've only looked through it! But it will at least bring in a little money."

"It won't even do that, for no one will want to print a bit by itself. The work is only of value as a whole."

She did not attach any importance to this.

"Come along," she said peremptorily, "we'll take them to the post."

Her intentions were excellent but misguided and, though experience had taught him how dangerous it was to take her advice, he let her have her way and they went out together.

On the stairs he noticed that she was limping. She had bought boots that were too tight, and in any case were of the high-heeled variety only worn at that time by fashionable prostitutes.

When they got out into the street she hurried on ahead to the post-office and he followed her. But when he saw her slight figure deformed by the many parcels she had insisted on carrying, saw her limping on her worn-down heels, he was seized by a feeling of revulsion.

It was the first time he had looked at her from behind and he began involuntarily to think of the wood-nymph, who seen from the front is an enchanting elf, but from behind looks like a trough.

The next moment he was overcome by remorse and was disgusted at himself and his own thoughts. Here, in this grim heat, was this little woman, carrying a heavy burden, on top of which she had written six long letters to the various editors, all for his sake. And she was limping!

But the brutal way in which she had treated his work, cut up a manuscript without having read it, chopped up a work of literature as a butcheress might her wares. . . .

Disgust got the upper hand again, followed once more by remorse that was mixed with the indefinable pain a man feels when he sees his beloved looking ugly, badly dressed, pitiable or absurd.

People in the street turned to look at her, especially when the wind billowed out her thin serge coat, cut like a dressing-gown, which swelled up like a balloon and distorted her beautiful figure.

He hurried forward to take the parcels, but she fended him off with a gesture of refusal and pressed on, happy, undaunted.

When she came out of the post-office she wanted to go and buy other, bigger boots, and he went with her. After half an hour of it she asked him to wait for her outside. When at last she joined him things went well for a short way along the street, but then she discovered that the new boots were also too tight.

"What a rotten shoemaker!"

"Perhaps, but I don't suppose he made the boots too tight especially for you. There must have been bigger ones!"

This was a poor way of beginning a conversation and when they sat down at a café table an uncomfortable silence ensued. They were sitting on opposite sides and could not help catching each other's eye. They tried to avoid doing so, but if they failed and were obliged to look at each other, they turned their heads aside.

"You would very much like to be in the Cloister now with your friends, wouldn't you?" she said.

"Well guessed!"

And it was true, but if at one second he had been able to transport himself there, at the next he would have wanted to get away again.

Their agitation increased and their eyes began to flash, but as she was intelligent, she realized that neither of them was to blame.

Cc

"Go out for a walk," she said. "We need to be apart for a while and you'll see that things will be better afterwards."

He entirely agreed with her and they parted without ill-feeling.

As he wandered beside the Alsterdam he felt his nerves beginning to sort themselves out and settle down. He refound his true self as a complete and independent entity. He was no longer sending out rays in all directions, but was concentrated, and his whole being was once again assembled within his own skin. How well he recognized these symptoms, of no particular significance, yet which defied all attempts to explain them. They remained a constantly recurring phenomenon which, though it resembled others experienced in other circumstances, was not of the same character.

However, when he began to find a positive pleasure in her absence, the idea that if he were permanently free of her he might experience an even greater degree of pleasure had no difficulty in creeping into his mind, and at the railway station he was suddenly struck by the thought:

"Shall I go now? In six hours I could be at the Cloister."

He sat down, ordered a glass of beer, lit a cigarette and meditated.

"If I go to England," he thought, "she'll have the upper hand, as she can speak the language. I shall be herded around like a deaf mute, and feel like an idiot among my literary friends, while she'll pop them straight into her pocket. I don't like the idea of that at all! The very fact that she's acting as my protectress with these German newspapers is humiliating enough." He had accepted a service from her. . . .

But in the midst of all this argufying he cut himself short, for he knew that no one remains intact if you begin to objectify and analyse them. He knew too that no one stands up to being seen from behind or judged in their absence. Suddenly a feeling of loneliness crept over him, a feeling too that he had been unfaithful, ungrateful. Something drew him back to her, and he rose from his seat and rapidly returned to the hotel.

When he entered their room, rather worked up and not a little sentimental, he was met by a ringing laugh, very prolonged and gay, like the aria of some garden songster. There she lay, dressed in a silk gown, curled up like an angora cat, eating sweets and sniffing a bottle of scent.

At this they both started to laugh as if they had seen something absurd in the street, something which had nothing to do with them.

They were soon established in Pimlico, a part of London just beyond Westminster, on the way to Chelsea. One visit had been paid and that had been the end. Everyone was away and the theatres were closed. The heat was tropical. It left you feeling like death from morning to evening and made the soul long to leave its penthouse and seek the cool of higher regions.

Approaching penury forced him to sit down unwillingly to write, but as he had used up most of his experiences he was obliged to attack a subject that was really forbidden. He did violence to his own feelings, overcame all discretion and began.

"I'm writing again," he told her. "We're saved!"

His wife came in and saw that one page was covered with writing.

An hour later she came in again, but now he was lying on the sofa, moaning.

"I can't do it! I'd rather we perished."

She left the room without saying a word, banging the door, which he then locked, and going to his portmanteau, he took from it a green canvas sack which contained a large number of sheets of paper, covered with figures and writing. This was the famous object known among his friends as "The Green Sack".

He had begun to be interested in chemistry and the other natural sciences even in his early schooldays. Later on he had studied medicine for two years and since that time had always followed developments in science. During the past two years he had systematically subjected the fundamental principles of chemistry and physics in particular to a critical investigation, and had come to the conclusion that no further progress would be made in these two sciences unless a new method was devised. He believed that he had discovered this method and proved by experiment that it would produce results. As he could neither write nor remain idle he was now filling up his time by theorizing and making calculations. As he always had a feeling that out of this green sack something fateful would emerge, which would affect his life either to his advantage or to his disadvantage, he kept the matter a secret from his wife.

When he had worked for a couple of hours he felt the usual uneasiness at not seeing his other self, and consequently went down to look for her.

He found her reading a book which she made a lame attempt to conceal when he entered. He saw by the unusual expression on her face that something ominous had come into their life.

"What are you reading?"

"Your last book!" she answered, putting a curious emphasis on the words.

It was the ruthless description of his first marriage, written in self-defence, and as a last testament, for he had intended to take his own life when he had finished writing it. For two years the sealed manuscript had lain deposited with a relative, and he had never intended to publish it. But in the spring of that year, under the pressure of circumstances, and because people had been trying so unjustly to annihilate him, both verbally and in the press, he had sold the book to a publisher.

Now it was out and had fallen into the very hands into which it never should have fallen. At first he wanted to snatch the book from her, but was restrained by the thought: "It has happened, therefore it was meant to happen!" and with a deadly calm, as if he had witnessed his own execution, which nothing could have prevented, he left the room.

At dinner he noticed the awful change that had come over his wife. The expression on her face was new; her eyes scrutinized the whole of his person, as if she were comparing him with the man in the book. He took it for granted that his sufferings would not rouse her compassion, for women always side with their own sex. What he did not succeed in grasping was, that in certain of her predecessor's characteristics, she recognized herself. Perhaps she had even found there a number of sharp retorts to remarks of hers, which he had hitherto refrained from answering, on that question which both husband and wife had instinctively avoided: the "Woman" question. There was no doubt that she had been made fully aware of her husband's views on her sex. She had of course known of them before, but in this book they were presented in such a brutal way that they could not fail to give her a mortal wound.

She did not say a word, but he could see by her face that his peace was at an end, and that this woman would never rest content until she had killed his honour and forced him to cut short his life. The only defence he had was his usual: be prepared for anything, endure things as long as you can, and then, when all else has failed, go your way and leave her alone to consume herself, for lack of any other form of nourishment for her hatred.

The next day she had hatched her egg and it proved to contain a basilisk.

With an expression which did not succeed in being innocent she announced that, as he could not work, they would have to consider ways of retrenching.

"Good," he replied.

First of all they must restrict themselves to one room. This meant that he would be denied any chance of being his own master, of withdrawing for a time, of collecting himself. From now onwards he would be locked up in the same cage with his tormentress, he would no longer be free to think and feel what he pleased, and above all he would be unable to use the Green Sack in his work.

"You can't work in any case!" she had remarked.

When dinner time arrived a plate of pork and a roll were placed before him.

"You don't insist on having soup," she said, "and no one can enjoy hot food in this heat."

Then she sat down to watch him.

"Aren't you going to eat?" he asked.

"No, I'm not hungry," she answered, and went on watching him.

He got up, picked up his hat and went out.

"Are you going out?" she asked. "I'm going too, so we can go together."

He strode on ahead and she followed. In order to torment her he chose the sunny side, that skirted a white wall, where the heat was intense and the reflected light made one's eyes smart. He then towed her out as far as Chelsea, where there was not a single house to offer any shade. She followed like an evil spirit.

When they got to the river he thought for a moment of pushing her into the water, but did not do so. He went down to the bank where lime barges were being unloaded, where steam winches were puffing out black smoke, where hawsers made walking hazardous. He hoped that she would fall and hurt herself, that harbourmen would bump into her. He wished that some docker would seize her in his arms and kiss her, why, he even felt he could look on unmoved while a drunken loafer raped her, so intense was his hatred, and hers.

He clambered over barrels and wheelbarrows, and walked through heaps of lime, but it was no use. He was driven to think again of jumping into the river and swimming to the opposite bank, but was deterred by the reflection that she too might be able to swim.

Finally he took a right about turn, like a bull pursued by a gadfly, and went towards Westminster. There the back streets were teeming with the strangest people, who resembled the terrifying figures one sees in a nightmare. He went into a church to scrub off the vermin as it were, but she went in after him, indefatigable, silent.

At last he was forced to go home, and once there he sat down in a chair and she sat opposite.

Then he realized what makes a man a murderer and determined to flee. But first he would have to send for some money.

Night came, and he thought it would give him a chance to collect his thoughts, to be his own master. He therefore pretended to be asleep, but she could hear by his breathing that this was not so.

"Are you awake?" she asked.

He was unwise enough to answer yes. After that they lay spying on each other to see who would fall asleep first. Finally he did.

Far on in the night he awoke, listened, and could hear by her breathing that she was asleep.

Then he stretched forth his soul, wrapped himself in darkness, and rejoiced in being able to think, unobserved by those cold, threatening eyes.

But she had not been asleep, and in the dark he heard her voice as before:

"Are you asleep?"

He sensed the vampire that had fastened on to his soul and was even keeping watch over his thoughts. Why should she spy on him if it were not that she feared the silent workings of his mind? Perhaps she could feel that he was lying there trying to work himself free of the meshes of her net, and would succeed if only he had a few hours of peace. But that was forbidden.

She herself gave up her sleep in order to torment him. She denied herself visits to the city, to libraries and museums, simply because she was determined not to leave him by himself.

The next day he asked her if she was still learning his language, as otherwise he would have to approach his former translators.

"Was I going to translate you?" she said scornfully. "I've better things to do than that."

"Why shouldn't you translate me rather than your trashy authors?"

"Take care, my friend," she snapped. "You're overrated, and a rude awakening from your dreams of greatness lies in store for you."

She said this in a tone which suggested that the opinion of all Europe was behind her, and it made some impression on him, for an author, even if well known, stands for nothing in his own eyes. Everything he is comes through the opinion other people have of his talent. He now felt the bond between them was broken. She hated and despised his work, which was his only justification for living, and by seeking to deprive him of courage and self-confidence, she had become his enemy.

There are only two ways of treating an enemy. You can either kill him, or refuse to take up the challenge and march off. He decided for the latter.

He had to hold out for a couple of days longer while he waited for money, but these two days were enough to increase his abhorrence. He was given the opportunity to see once again cold, calculated spite, combined with malicious joy at the success of her schemes, all a woman's pettiness, meanness and treachery, but this time on a grander scale. And, as if she knew that he could not escape for lack of money, she let him see that she regarded him as her prisoner, which he was not.

The room looked like a pigsty and the food was especially prepared to make it repulsive. Disorder and squalor reigned supreme. He felt as if he were in hell, and thought with regret of his solitary attic, where there had always been perfect order, in spite of the disordered state of his affairs. Only two months had passed since the wedding, but they no longer smiled, and even conversation between them had ceased. Love was changed to mad hatred, and he began to think that she was ugly.

On their last day together he had to speak out or burst.

"You were beautiful as long as I loved you. Perhaps my love made you beautiful, and not only to my eyes. Now you're the ugliest and most worthless person I ever remember meeting in my life."

To which she answered:

"I know that I've never been so horrible to anyone as I am to you, and I can't tell you why."

"I can tell you why," he said. "You hate me because I'm a man and your husband."

He had packed up his bag and she knew that he was going. But when the moment of parting approached—a parting which she supposed would be forever—behold hatred melted, and love appeared on the scene again! Her tenderness and consideration knew no bounds. They talked of the future as if they would soon meet again. She gave him good advice in a motherly but submissive tone, and seemed resigned, as one confronted by an inflexible fate which had ordained that they must part for the present. As they drove along the main street to the station in an open cab, the day being sunny, she kissed him repeatedly. Passers-by laughed at them, but when he saw the police taking notice of the affectionate couple he grew alarmed:

"Be careful! In this country you can be put in prison for being too demonstrative in public."

"I don't care," she answered. "I love you so much."

In this mood of defiant tenderness he once more thought her sublime, and they agreed to meet again in a week at the latest.

His plan was to go to the island of Rügen where his helpful friend Ilmarinen was having a seaside holiday. He would assist him to put his affairs in order. Then he would rent a flat, and in fourteen days at the latest, at the very latest, she would join him.

"Don't you see now that we can't depend on that hatred?"

"No, but upon love!"

"It looks as if it had triumphed."

Their parting at the station was heart-rending, and when at last he was sitting alone in his compartment he experienced only the desolation of loss. The happiness of release, of which he had so recently dreamt, was not in evidence at all. All memory of her wickedness had been blown away.

He went from London to Hamburg in the hope that he would there find friends who would help him to push on to Rügen, but his plans were bewitched. Everyone was away in the country or absent for some other reason. He was therefore forced to put up at an hotel and resort to telegrams. The first was to Ilmarinen, but he had no money, and a similar answer arrived from Berlin.

This made him feel that he had been caught in a trap and overpowered. Cholera had raged in Hamburg the previous year, and they were expecting it again this year if the heat returned, which was just what had happened. Thus, if he did not get away quickly he might expect not death, to which he was indifferent, but quarantine.

With the threatened outbreak of cholera hanging over him and no one to whom he could talk, the days passed slowly and painfully. Helpless as he was, and in a permanent state of fury with the invisible power that seemed to have a grudge against him, he became paralysed, and no longer dared to lift a finger to change his fate, so much did he fear failure and the betrayal of his hopes. In order to pass the time he sat down to calculate molecular weights, and worked with figures from morning till night. Nevertheless the days remained interminably long, and he became obsessed with the idea that he would never get away from this dreadful city, where nothing but buying and selling went on. The impression that he would end his days in this horrible hotel room grew so vivid, that he unpacked his belongings and began to ornament the chest-of-drawers with photographs of his children and other relatives.

Loneliness and misery had the effect of prolonging time, so that he began to imagine that he was a citizen of Hamburg. He momentarily forgot his past, forgot that he was married, or that he had ever lived anywhere else.

He looked upon himself as a prisoner, but horribly enough, one who did not know what crime he had committed, who had sentenced him, or who was acting as his gaoler. But invisible in the filthy waters of the canals the black spectre of cholera lay in wait for him. He asked the waiter three times a day for news of the cholera, but always got the same answer: "We don't know for sure."

At last a letter arrived from his wife. She loudly proclaimed her loss, her love, and her uneasiness. She wanted to know where he was. He replied in the same strain and bellowed with rage at the fate that had parted them.

On the morning of the fifth day he saw in the paper that his Danish friend from the Cloister[9] was living half an hour's journey by train from Hamburg. If only he had known this before he need never have endured so much suffering. As he could not pay the hotel bill he made up his mind to leave without notice, and not to return. His friend would give him money which he would send to the hotel and they could then send his things on after him. He boarded the train feeling like a released prisoner, bestowed a compassionate glance on Hamburg, as if he forgave it his injuries, but promised himself that he would never again honour the place by visiting it unless he were obliged.

Half an hour in the train put him in a good humour and his mouth began to water at the thought of being able to give vent to his annoyance. Perhaps he would even touch up the whole story of his martyrdom so that it sounded like a comic incident. Blessed light-heartedness returned and it seemed to him that he must really be one of fortune's favourites, since he was so unexpectedly to meet one of his fellow cloisterers.

He stopped outside the pleasant little inn, where the host was standing at the door, and asked if Mr XX was there.

"No, he left this morning."

"Where did he go?"

"To Denmark!"

Back in the train after a three-hour wait, which had given the smart from the blow time to subside, he thought:

"There's something wrong here, something unnatural. This isn't the true logic of events. This must undoubtedly be something else!"

When he saw the spires of Hamburg reappearing all his old hatred was aroused, and this increased to unbelievable proportions when he saw a stretcher on the station platform.

"Now the cholera is here!" he thought. "Fourteen days quarantine!"

But there was no cholera. That in itself was a great piece of good fortune which, however, he was unable to enjoy, as he now became convinced that it would break out the day his money arrived. Moreover, he also reckoned that he would never get away from Hamburg for the following reason. The money would be so slow in arriving that the hotel bill—which would increase in geometrical progression—would swallow it all up, leaving nothing for the journey. In this way a state of perpetual motion would come about which might very well continue until doomsday.

When the money did actually arrive two days later his calculations were shown to be more or less correct. He paid his bill, left the hotel in a cab, and drove to the station. There he had to pay the cabby and also a brusher,* who had followed him from the hotel to demand a tip, and to hand him a bill for out-of-pocket expenses, probably invented. When he got to the ticket office and asked the fare, he found he was two marks short, and therefore had to return to the hotel.

It is surely unnecessary to dwell on all the details of this man's suffering in order to give the reader a living impression of what he endured. Suffice to say that the silence cure lasted for several more days, and that he eventually got away before the cholera had time to break out.

His object in making this journey to Rügen was partly to get away from woman, and enjoy masculine society, and partly, with Ilmarinen's help, to put his affairs in order. But perhaps his main reason was to give himself a chance to talk. This was no doubt why fate, or whoever it might be, had condemned him to absolute silence in Hamburg, for "Fate" always sought out his secret longings in order to annihilate them. When he finally arrived in Rügen, expecting to be able to talk to his heart's content for half the night, he found Ilmarinen changed, cool, and embarrassed. The fact was that the latter had heard that his friend had married the daughter of wealthy parents— which was quite true—and he was therefore unable to understand the reason for this sudden onset of poverty. When the new arrival asked if they could sup together the Finn excused himself on the grounds that he had been invited to a birthday-party.

"You see, I'm staying here with Laïs's oldest friend, the Swede, who was in love with her, the man who turned up just at the end."

"Is he here?"

"Yes, he's been here ever since Laïs and the Russian, who has abandoned his helpmate and his child, got engaged."

* A man employed by an hotel to brush clothes and shoes.

"So this is where he is? He probably hates me, doesn't he?"

"To tell you the truth he does. Your presence here will annoy him."

So he had to spend the first evening alone, by himself, after a long period of being alone, *à deux* with a woman, and then alone with himself.

He felt as if he were living under a curse. This insignificant, uneducated Ilmarinen, whom he had lifted up from nothing, and introduced into his circle. Whom he had fed and sheltered, in exchange for the small errands he had run to theatres and publishers, which had been an honour for a young, unknown writer, and also an advantage, as they had provided him with an opportunity of making known his own work. Now the famulus was throwing over his teacher because he did not think there was anything more to be gained, and because he thought he could now manage on his own.

The days that followed were so horrible that he again began to think that this could not be the natural order of things, but that the black hand must be interfering in his destiny.

Since this third-class bathing-resort had but one inn he was obliged to sit down to table with his fellow-countryman—who ascribed to him the loss of Laïs—and with Ilmarinen, who thought he was done for and therefore adopted a haughty attitude towards him.

In addition to this, a sort of overcooked pigswill was served up, so that you left the table hungry and went hungry all day. Everything was adulterated, even the beer. And as for the meat, the host's family boiled all the goodness out of it for themselves first, all the guests got were the sinews and the bones, just the sort of food you give to dogs. Glances of half-concealed antagonism from his unfortunate countryman did not serve to make the imagined pleasures of the table any greater.

He had been there a week without hearing a word from his wife in London. At first life on the island—by contrast to that in the Hamburg hotel—seemed to him endurable, but when one day he woke up and began to reflect upon his situation, he saw that it was absolutely infernal.

He had been given an attic room where the sun blazed down on the leads which were only a foot above his head. Sixteen years previously he had left the leaden chamber five floors up, in which he had lived as a bachelor, and moved to a flat, which he had entered as a married man. Since that time one of his nightmares had been to find himself creeping up those five flights to his bachelor room, where all the misery and dirt of an unmarried man's existence awaited him. Now he was again in an attic room, and again a bachelor, in spite of being married. It was like the punishment that follows repeated warnings, but what law he had broken he did not know.

Then too the part of Rügen in which they lived consisted of loose, glistening sand, which grew so hot under the midsummer sun that it did not cool down at night. This first led him to think of the bags of hot sand that peasants use in cases of pneumonia, but later, after he had searched his memory for a long time, the picture of Dante's Hell rose before him, in which the blasphemers lie outstretched on hot sand. However, as he did not believe himself to know that a good God existed, he felt that his blasphemies should go unavenged.

After a week of walking in deep sand he perceived the hellishness in the torment of taking one step forward and half a step back, of having to lift up your foot six inches in order to advance, and most of all perhaps, of feeling yourself sinking into the ground like the girl who trod on the loaf of bread.* Never to have firm ground under your feet, never to be able to stride out freely and keep pace with your thoughts, but to have to drag yourself along like an old man, that was indeed to

---

* The girl in a folk-tale who threw a loaf of bread on to swampy ground in order to save wetting her feet. When she trod on it the loaf sank into the swamp and she with it.

be in hell. On top of this was the heat that never abated. The air in his attic burned him by day, and at night, when he lay naked in bed, he was grilled by the leads on the roof.

You might have thought that the nearness of the sea would have quenched the fire, but even this was cunningly calculated, in keeping with all the rest. Ever since his youth he had always dived in head-first when he bathed, as he could not bear crawling into water. Here too a horrible and recurring dream played a part in the spiteful game. He was in the habit of dreaming that he was overheated and felt that he must get into the sea. The sea was there, but it was so shallow that he could not dive, and continued to be so shallow when he crawled out, that he could not duck his head.

This was precisely the situation here.

"Have I come to this place to see all my bad dreams come true and staged for me?" he asked himself, and with good cause!

Ilmarinen became more impudent each day. He kept asking when his wife would arrive and clearly believed, after fourteen days had elapsed, that she had thrown him over. Laïs's friend was of course pleased, and this made his hell complete, for there was naturally something very ignominious about the position of discarded husband.

Relations with England had also assumed a threatening aspect, so that he was not sure himself whether he was married or divorced. One letter would proclaim undying love, the pangs of separation and the torment of longing. They were Hero and Leander on either side of a sea, and if only she had been able to swim, she would soon have been with her Leander, even at the risk of floating on to his island as a corpse. In the next letter she would tell him that she was thinking of opening a theatre in London, for which she was trying to raise capital, but she could not find the money for a steamship ticket.

In a third letter she told him that she was ill. It was full of reproaches for a husband who had left his sick wife in want in a foreign country. (She did not mention the fact that she herself was rich!)

A fourth letter said that she was in the convent of The English Ladies where she had been at school, and where she had now regained her youth and her innocence, and was cursing the wretchedness of the world and that hell, marriage.

It was impossible to reply sensibly to all this, for the letters rained down like hail and crossed each other in the post, so that when he had sent off a tender letter he would receive an abusive one in reply to a previous letter that had been sharp, or vice versa. Their misunderstanding was complete and senseless, but when he broke off negotiations, she started to send telegrams.

This witches' brew lasted for a month, and he began to look back on the hours in Hamburg, now a happy memory, as a period which, compared with the present, had been indescribably delightful.

Then came a letter from his sister-in-law which seemed like a release from the gallows. She invited him to her father's villa outside Salzburg. His wife in London had received a similar invitation, so it was near Salzburg that they were to be reunited.

Prepared for anything, even for the worst, he now entered upon that phase of his ordeal which would produce the most curious of all his metamorphoses. From being a father and a husband he would once more become a child, be grafted on to a family, and get a new father and mother in place of those he had lost many years previously. A factor which would help to increase the confusion was that his father and mother-in-law had been separated for seven years, but now, on account of their daughter's marriage, they were to meet again. He had thus become a sort of hyphen, but as the daughter, now his wife, had also been on bad terms with her father, it seemed likely that this family reunion would prove to be a feast of multiple reconciliation.

His past experience did not suggest that much good ever

came of family reconciliations, and since his own slate was not clean, the idyll beside Mondsee that loomed ahead looked to him like a snake-pit. How was he going to explain the unnatural parting from his bride of only eight weeks' standing? To offer money difficulties as an excuse would be the worst thing he could do, for a son-in-law in money difficulties is an impostor, or a person who hopes to inherit your property.

As he approached the place of rendezvous he grew nervous, but, as usual, finally succeeded in restoring his courage by looking at the matter from the writer's point of view: "If I don't come out of this with honour, I shall at least get a chapter for my novel."

What might happen to him could also be looked at from the point of view of the innocent martyr: "Let's see how far Fate will carry her spite, and how much I can stand!"

When the train stopped at the elegant little branch-line station he looked out for a face that was seeking his.

A young lady, holding a well-dressed child by the hand, came up to him, asked his name, and introduced herself as the French governess, employed by his brother-in-law, who had been sent to act as his guide.

A beautiful white village, the houses of which had steeply sloping roofs and green shutters, lay in a deep valley-basin, which was surrounded by small alps, and enclosed a pretty lake. On the outskirts of the village, towards the shores of the lake, stood the villa. Along the road under the lime-trees, a white-haired, bare-headed woman came to meet him. She embraced him and bade him welcome. This was his bride's mother, and he instantly became aware of the miraculous transference of emotions which an act as simple as that of marriage had the power to effect. This was his mother, and he was her son.

"I knew you long before you met my daughter," said the old lady in the quavering voice of a religious fanatic, "and in a way I've been expecting you! There is much that's evil in your writings, but your immorality is childish. Your sentiments about women are correct, and your godlessness isn't your fault, for He has not wanted to know you, but you'll see, He will soon come to you. You've married a worldling, but you won't put up with her for long when you realize that she'll drag you down among the banalities of life. Once you are alone you'll find again the vocation of your youth."

She spoke these words like a sibyl, with a complete lack of embarrassment, as if another being were speaking through her, and for this reason she had no fear of saying too much.

When the conversation subsequently returned to earth he seized the opportunity of enquiring after his father-in-law, whose absence surprised him. He had not arrived, but was expected the following evening.

His sister-in-law now appeared, but her behaviour was cold, ominous, and conventional. He had hoped that her presence would give him support, for he had believed her to be a friend, but now he saw this hope toppling, especially as she was intending to depart before her father arrived.

They did not talk much about his wife, and no one appeared to know whether she meant to come or not.

Had he been enticed into an ambush, he asked himself, and was he now going to be court-martialled? Had his wife in England brought an accusation against him, or how was he to assess the situation? A mother-in-law who practically urged him to have a divorce, and who spoke ill of her own child! That was highly original to say the least of it.

Meanwhile he was conducted into the villa, a magnificent two-storey stone house with innumerable rooms, all filled with antique furniture, porcelain, and valuable trinkets. This house, which could easily have accommodated two large families, was only used by its master for six weeks of the year when he took his holiday. Otherwise it stood empty. This suggested wealth, and induced the son-in-law to imagine that here at least people would not talk of poverty, its causes, or how to cure it.

He passed the day in conversation with his mother-in-law, who was tirelessly attentive and kind. She was capable at any moment of leading the conversation to a discussion of serious subjects, and she was a religious mystic, who saw the guiding hand of providence in everything. There was consequently a certain tolerance about her attitude to life, since she believed that what people did was as good as predestined.

In order to take the most usual way of making himself agreeable he tentatively adopted her point of view, and dug up from his past things which seemed to foreshadow present events.

"Do you know," he said, "that Austria has several times appeared to me as an apparition? Some years ago I was visiting a friend at Alpenzell, in Switzerland. We were snowed up and could only look out of the windows, but whenever we did so we saw a blue-black wall of rock in the distance.

"On the third day curiosity drove me to ask: 'What's that blue-blackness that pursues me everywhere? I see it from whichever window I look.' 'That's Austria!' he answered.

"So that was Austria! I wanted to know what lay behind that dark wall. I dreamed of something beautiful, longed to see what it was, for I felt sure that it was something which would influence my destiny. On days when rain clouds gathered, the black wall drew nearer.

"I also lived in Bavaria once, close to Bregenz. For half a year my morning walk led me as far as a bridge, half of which was painted white and blue, and the other half yellow and black. I knew immediately that this must be the frontier, and when I got home and people asked where I'd been I answered: 'I've been to Austria.'

"Then the children wanted to come too and see 'where the lapwing lived'. You see we've a nursery rhyme in Sweden which runs:

'Where does the lapwing live?
In Austria.
What does she do there?
She lays her eggs.
How many clutches?
Baskets full.'

"So I took the children down to the bridge, which they stormed, and standing with one foot in each country they cried: 'Now I'm in Bavaria, now I'm in Austria.'

"I got no further than the frontier that time. Now I know where the lapwing lives and I've seen what lies behind the black mountain. It's very strange. In a certain sense I'm an Austrian, one of those imperialists against whom the Swedes fought in the Thirty Years War!"

"Yes," answered the old lady. "I told you, didn't I, that I'd known that you'd come? that one of that savage people whom I'd never seen would come and carry off my daughter. But you can imagine that my husband wasn't happy about it. He's a very violent person, but good at heart. You'll have a hard time of it with him, but it won't last long if only you don't answer back. It's at any rate fortunate that your wife hasn't arrived, for he has a bone to pick with her too."

"With her too?"

"Well yes, but don't misunderstand me. It's not very serious. Everything will turn out all right if only his rage is allowed to blow itself out."

"I can see that there's bound to be a storm, but I can't see why. I acted in good faith and everyone has the right to be the victim of misfortunes that he hasn't brought upon himself."

"Certainly, but everything will turn out all right, you'll see."

At last evening came and he was taken to his room. This had three windows, each facing in a different direction. There were no blinds and the curtains could not be drawn together. He felt like someone under surveillance, or a person in quarantine under observation, and when he got into bed he found himself staring at his father-in-law's bust. The face did not look kind, rather the reverse, and illuminated from below it assumed all kinds of alarming expressions.

"And tomorrow," he thought, "I'm going to be put in my place, by a stranger whom I've never met; be knocked about like a schoolboy because I've had misfortunes. Ah well, I must accept this too, along with all the rest."

The following morning he awoke feeling quite definitely that he was in a snake-pit into which Satan had tempted him. This being the case he knew there was no chance of escape and stayed where he was. He went out to botanize and look at the landscape, and succeeded in working himself up into the irresponsible frame of mind of the creative artist, which enabled him to think only about what was exciting in the situation. "This is a scene which no one has acted before. It's mine, even if it's going to make my skin smart."

Dinner time arrived. The atmosphere at the table, where his father-in-law's seat remained threateningly empty, was certainly not merry.

After dinner he went up to his room to calm his nerves, but very soon the arrival of the Privy Counsellor was announced.

He went downstairs, smiling and shivering by turns.

On the veranda stood a man who looked about forty. He was youthfully dressed and had the sparkling eyes of a young man.

What sort of expression he himself was wearing the son-in-law could not guess, but his instincts must have worked to his advantage, for the old gentleman greeted him with respect, asked him to forgive his late arrival, said polite things about his writings, and invited him to sit down, all the time using the formal mode of address. He had just come from seeing the Kaiser at Ischl (the Kaiser! Oh!), and talked for a long time of this and that, clearly with the intention of observing his son-in-law, who sat silent and attentive. He then turned to his wife and asked her if she had entertained their guest suitably, turned again to him and asked if there was anything he wanted.

Without a moment's hesitation he rose, went up to his father-in-law and said:

"There's only one thing I want. I want my wife's father to call me by my christian name."

The old man's eyes flashed with pleasure. He opened his arms and the sceptic again felt the emotion he had experienced on meeting his mother-in-law. The invisible ties of blood had been joined. He was sincerely affected and was once more transformed into a child.

"You're a good fellow," said the old man. "I can look you straight in the eye." And with that he kissed his cheek.

"But," he continued, "you've got Maria now, and I hear you know what you've got. You must make the best of it and never come complaining to me. If you can't manage her you must put up with her. You've got what you wanted, and you're welcome to it."

Thereupon they drank coffee and conversed as relatives or very old friends. Presently the old gentleman said he wanted to go fishing. He went off to change and returned wearing a summer suit of white cashmere, which made him seem younger than ever. The trousers looked as if they had belonged to his court costume, and you could see the marks where the gold braid had been, but the bohemian from that low haunt, the Cloister, was impressed. Moreover the cigars he offered were a present from the Kaiser!

And to think that this Privy Counsellor, who had dined with the Kaiser, was now going off to fish with an anarchist, and one with a rather tender conscience too, for not so long ago he had been thinking what fine fellows the Viennese anarchists were when they blew up a few strong-boxes. How comical! But

then the old gentleman himself talked understandingly about
Ibsen, about modern movements, and about Scandinavian
literature in general. He also knew all about his son-in-law's
horrible activities, so the latter did not think there was any
reason to feel embarrassed. In fact he seemed to approve of his
views on the "Woman" question, and said so in the following
words:

"Yes, you've written everything I should like to have
written myself."

This was perhaps not meant entirely seriously, but it was
what he said.

By this time they had reached the stream.

"Have you ever fished for trout before?" asked the old
gentleman.

"Never."

"In that case perhaps you'd better just help me."

This help consisted in being ready to scoop up the fish with a
landing net, and in extracting the hook without damaging the
artificial fly. As everything needs practice the son-in-law was
butter-fingered and got snubbed. But he was entering into his
new role so thoroughly that he found this quite natural, just as
natural as it had been to take his own children fishing.

When the sun went down they abandoned the sport and the
son-in-law was granted the honour of carrying home the
fishing-rods, the landing net, and the fish.

The evening was a happy one, and the old gentleman telegraphed money to London with instructions that the young
lady should return immediately.

"I'm doing this for your sake," he said to his son-in-law.

In other words she had not been summoned before, and he
been enticed there by the methods used to capture singing-
birds!

"I think I came out of that quite well," he said to his mother-
in-law when he was saying goodnight.

"The worst is probably over, but you're not at the end yet."

"Why, is he intending to give us both a beating at the same time?"

His troubles were far from being over. The following morning he had a letter from London in which his wife said goodbye to him for ever (Lord Byron) because, in choosing between her and her parents, he had preferred them.

As he had had no choice, this was simply a piece of nonsense she was using to cover something else.

In a letter to her mother she said the same thing, equally violently, and added: "Good luck to you."

Her mother interpreted it as follows:

"She's jealous. She's afraid that you'll tell tales about her and that we shall listen to you. She's so domineering that she can't bear even parental control. If you become good friends with her father and mother she'll be in the position of a child to you too."

He thought this was very likely, but not entirely normal. She ought to have been glad that he had won her parents over, and achieved a reconciliation.

Her father grew angry and took the matter seriously. He telegraphed an ultimatum and demanded an answer. Clouds began to gather and the fun was at an end.

As the husband dreaded the thought of a conflict on the spot he sent a telegram saying:

"I'm going to Berlin. If you don't join me there I shall petition for a divorce."

But as he had to wait for an answer he stayed where he was.

That night he did not sleep, for the situation was hopelessly bizarre. If she accepted the suggestion of a divorce how was he going in an instant to cut the ties of relationship that had been joined? Who then was the man who had just entered the family in the character of a relation and been taken into their confidence? What would the old couple think? He would have to find a motive for such a sudden break.

The following morning a telegram from Holland arrived from his young wife. Everything seemed destined to be as crazy as possible, and this telegram was so badly phrased that it could be read to mean: "I'm coming to you," but equally well: "I'm coming to Berlin to meet you there."

This document became a veritable apple of discord, and for three days the parents-in-law and the husband interpreted it backwards and forwards and this way and that, but no young wife arrived. They listened for the steam-whistle and went down to meet trains. They came back and started to interpret all over again. No one had any peace of mind and they could not carry on a conversation without twisting their heads about and listening.

After two days of this the father-in-law lost patience. The affair had another aspect which was important to him: the scandal! The whole village knew that the son-in-law was there and that his wife was lost. It knew too that a search was being made for her by telegram.

The father-in-law therefore spent all day shut up in his room and now plunged ruthlessly into a discussion of money matters.

"Have you a reliable income?"

"About as unreliable as it's possible for a writer to have."

"Very well then, you'll have to do as other people do and write for the papers."

"No paper will print my articles."

"Then write so that they will print them."

This was more than a sceptic and a quietist had any right to put up with, but he did, and held his peace, firmly determined to take a guitar and travel around as an indifferent street-singer rather than sell his soul.

The old gentleman had himself been a novelist and poet in his youth, but he had thrown up the sponge in the struggle to

earn a living for his family. He would therefore have been
justified in saying: "You must do as I did." But he knew by
experience what such a struggle meant and, suddenly seized by
compassion, he began to utter friendly and encouraging words.
A moment later his justifiable suspicions again got the upper
hand and, as the memory of his own sacrifices made him bitter,
he felt the need to trample on one whose misfortunes had put
him under his feet. Moreover, when he saw how his son-in-law
kept silent and put up with everything, his evil genius whispered to him that this man, who could endure so much, was only
able to do so because he was hoping to become his heir. He
therefore began to talk about King Lear, about ungrateful
daughters who left their seventy-year-old father to his own
devices and merely waited for his death, while at the same time
they bereft him of his honour.

Thus the day passed, and if the son-in-law withdrew, he was
again sent for to receive another whipping.

As he knew how to think and suffer with and through others,
he made no effort to defend himself. Instead he imagined himself in the position of an old man, discarded, despised, and
abandoned by his children.

"You're right," he said, "but all the same I don't feel I'm to
blame."

On the evening of the third day after the telegram had been
sent to London his mother-in-law came up to see him.

"You must leave early tomorrow morning, for he can't bear
the sight of you any longer!"

"Good! I'll go."

"And if Maria comes she won't be received."

"Have you ever seen a person in a situation like the one I'm
in?"

"No, and my husband says the same thing. It upsets him to
see a deserving person like yourself in such a humiliating
position. He suffers on your behalf, and he doesn't want to

suffer. You know how I regard the matter. This is not anyone's fault, nor is it the fault of circumstances. You're fighting against someone who is hunting you, and will go on hunting you, until you're so tired, that you'll be forced to seek peace in the only place where peace is to be found. You'll always have a friend in me, even if you are divorced from my daughter, and I shall follow your fate with my best wishes and my prayers!"

Left alone in his room he began to feel his spirits rising at the thought that the morrow would see the end of this misery, which was among the worst he had ever experienced.

In order to have something fresh to think about he picked up a newspaper. It was the official or Court newspaper that his father-in-law edited. He ran his eye rapidly over the front page and down to the literary section, where an article attracted his attention. He read it supposing that the old gentleman must have written it. He soon noticed that it revealed wide reading, cocksure opinions, and a confident and refined style. What surprised him was its antagonism to everything that was modern, including things Scandinavian, while German literature—which at that time was practically non-existent— was declared most emphatically to be the literature that was setting the tone, and leading the civilized world. Germany always in the van!

When he had finished reading it he saw that it was signed by his wife.

Now he had promised his wife that he would never read her articles, and he had kept his promise in order to avoid the intrusion of literary discussions into his married life. That she seemed to hold views quite unlike those she daily advertised could only be due to the fact that she had to write "so that she got printed".

What a double life this woman must be leading if she could appear in the radical circles of Berlin as an anarchist, and in the official newspaper of Vienna as an old-fashioned conservative. How was it possible to switch generations in this way? He did not know and was too tired to try to find out. But it explained why she found it impossible to understand how he could be idle in a world full of pens and paper.

And what was he to think of the business ability, the worldly wisdom, and the old-fashioned style, things that seemed more indicative of a bald head and glasses than of a beautiful, laughing young girl, who could lie on a sofa and eat sweets like an odalisque.

It was really surprising how extraordinarily complicated people could be! Interesting at any rate! Worth bearing in mind!

He fell asleep feeling that he was considerably the wiser for the experience.

At seven o'clock he got up, having been awakened by the man who was going to carry his luggage. As his mother-in-law had told him that the train left shortly before eight, he did not hurry, but dressed at leisure and went into the garden where he met her.

They were just standing talking about the course his future was likely to take when they heard the roar of a brutal voice from above. It came from a window on the first floor. It was the old gentleman.

"Haven't you gone yet?"

"No, the train doesn't leave until a quarter to eight."

"What idiot told you that?"

As it was his mother-in-law who had told him he was naturally unable to say who the idiot was.

"Be off down to the station then, and find out from the time-table what time the next train leaves."

When he hesitated he heard a brief "Pish" like the crack of a horse-whip.

He was now quite clear as to what he must do, pressed his mother-in-law's hand, and departed.

They must have seen by his firm tread, so unlike that with which he had approached the lion's den, that his feet were now leading him out into the world, away, but would never bring him back, for he heard the old man's voice again, but now the tone was ingratiating and complaining:

"Axel!"

It pierced the heart of the man marching away, but he had got into his stride, and without turning round he walked on.

Walked down to the station, pretended to look at a time-table, asked when the next train left without hearing the answer, left the station, saw by the sun where the north-west lay, and took the next high-road in that direction, all this as calmly as if he were following a long-prepared plan.

He soon found himself in the country, alone, homeless, with no luggage, no overcoat, nothing but the stick in his hand.

He was not angry with anyone. The old man had been right, and his last cry still rang in his son-in-law's ears like a plea for forgiveness for his bad temper. In fact he could only feel guilty about this man to whom he had brought ignominy and pain. Yet he was still unable to bring himself to admit that he had been to blame. He had only done what he ought and what he could.

His plan was to walk as far as a station, take a train from there to Salzburg, telegraph for his luggage, and go on to Berlin.

"It would be laughable," he said to himself, "if only it were not so tragic for the old people. What lies ahead looks difficult, but I've come through worse things. A knight of the road, that's what I am. Good. No need to have any more pretensions to honour and glory and that sort of thing. At any rate it's soothing to have nothing to lose. Hurrah!"

He took the next village like a Swedish warrior of the Thirty Years War, ordered wine and tobacco at the inn, and grew so light-hearted that he had to chat to the landlord. Then he marched on again.

But now and then he fell into a sentimental mood, thought of his mother-in-law's words about the wild hunt, had to admit that something was amiss, for he had never before seen anyone have such bad luck, and if other people noticed it too, then it must be true. Still, that did not really matter. He had had bad luck ever since he was a child. "Cast out this bondwoman's son" rang in his ears. "His hand will be against every man and every man's hand against him."

Anyhow! Fancy putting a human being in such a situation! He would not himself have treated an enemy with such hellish cruelty.

Meanwhile, he reached Salzburg, then Munich, and quite soon Berlin.

It was evening and he sent a messenger to the family with whom his wife usually stayed. As she had not come to Mondsee she was presumably in Berlin. On the visiting-card which he despatched, he had simply written: "A rather unusual question. Where is my wife?"

No man born of woman who has not waited impatiently for an hour and a half on the edge of a pavement can have any idea of how long that time can be. But his vigil was made shorter by the hope that, after eight days of the silence cure in Hamburg, five weeks of solitary confinement on Rügen, and a week of the seventh hell in Mondsee, he would once again see his wife.

However, after an hour and a half the messenger returned with another visiting-card on which was written: "She left this morning for Mondsee, hoping to meet you there!"

Bang! Bang! Bang!

"Now things are really going too far even if it's an intrigue," he said to himself. "If a situation like this was used in a novel, the reader would throw down the book and exclaim: 'No, this is really laying it on a bit *too* thick!' And yet it's not funny enough to be farcical."

His next thought was:

"My poor unfortunate wife! She's walking straight into the lion's den! Now she'll get a beating!"

His father-in-law's rage was said to know no bounds, and on his last day at Mondsee his mother-in-law had said:

"If she comes now he'll hit her!"

He therefore telegraphed to the old lady to prepare her for her daughter's arrival and to beg for clemency.

It would be four days before his wife could get back. In order to avoid walking the streets of Berlin and having his honeymoon-trip reported in the papers, he settled down in a village on the outskirts of the city where the Savage and his family lived.

At the inn there he was subjected to the same regime of pig-swill that he had experienced in Rügen. After two days of it his strength was so far reduced that he was as weak as if he had been ill with typhus. You chewed until your jaws were tired, and if you went hungry to table, you left it both hungry and exhausted.

The Savage was not at all like himself. His own disappointed hopes had made him splenetic, and he suffered from the illusion that the well-known author's pitiful predicament gave him a favourable opportunity of rehabilitating himself. His sympathy was therefore effusive but carefully calculated to give pain, and when Axel tried to tell him about his adventures on his honeymoon, he stared at him in such a way that he hastily cut short his story, for fear of being treated as a liar.

The village was a swampy mass of overgrown tree-stumps and he found it depressing, though he did not know why. But when he walked along one of the streets, he was surprised to see people standing by the windows secretly looking at the stranger with wild, distraught eyes, and then hiding themselves furtively behind the curtains.

This made him uneasy, and he began to wonder if someone had been spreading abroad the false rumour that he was mad.

When he asked the Savage what it meant, the latter answered:

"Don't you know where you are?"

This question sounded very strange, and might be meant to suggest that in his bewildered state he had lost consciousness.

"I'm in Pankow," he replied, in order to avoid revealing his suspicions.

"Don't you know what Pankow is?"

"No."

"Well, it's just one big madhouse, where the inhabitants make their living by looking after lunatics in their homes," the Savage told him with a laugh.

After that he asked no more questions, but wondered to himself: "Have I been enticed here, have they got me in a trap so that they can observe what I do?" And he had good cause to be suspicious, for the same thing had happened to him before.

His existence now became a single-minded effort to show himself to be commonplace in his thoughts and staid in his behaviour, so that nobody would be able to see anything "unusual" about him. He did not dare to throw out an original remark, and every time he felt tempted to say anything about his honeymoon he pinched his own knee. But the constant anxiety that he was being observed weighed upon him so heavily that he saw watchful eyes everywhere, and thought that questions had a catch in them where none existed. In his over-sensitive state it seemed to him that the whole village exuded the sick humours of the mad, and he feared that he too would become insane. Yet he did not want to move, partly because he was convinced that he would be arrested on the station, and partly because he had told his wife to meet him in Pankow.

A letter had in fact arrived from Mondsee in which his

Dc

mother-in-law told him how uneasy and sorrowful his dis-
appearance had made them. His father-in-law, who probably
knew very well what he himself would have done in the
unfortunate man's place, had instantly begun to think of suicide,
and had wept profusely. The shores of the lake and the forest
had been searched. . . .

He interrupted his reading at this point and his conscience
pricked him. The kind old man had wept! What a dreadful
fate his must be if others could see it in this light!

But now Maria had come back, and if only he stayed on in
Pankow they would soon see each other, for she loved him.
That was a bright spot and it gave him strength to endure a
hellish place, where everyone looked askance at everyone else
to see if they were mad.

But his two last days there were to bring with them new
instruments of torture.

The Russian, Popoffsky, from the Cloister, was expected to
dinner. A joyful Axel B. went to meet the train to welcome his
most faithful friend, the person who had understood him best
and who, though poor himself, had ingratiated himself with
rich men in order to get for his friend the help he could not get
for himself.

But the man he met was a stranger, who looked at him coldly
and treated him as if he had never met him before. No smile
of recognition, no questions as to how he was and, above all,
no references to the past.

After dinner he took the Savage aside and asked:

"Is the Russian angry with me?"

"Angry? No! But you must realize that as he's now married
to Laïs. . . ."

"Married?"

"Yes, and he doesn't want to be reminded that she was once
your lady friend."

"I can understand that, but I'm not responsible for the fact that I was her friend before she had any idea that the Russian existed."

"No, of course not, but you've gossiped about her. . . ."

"Only in the way that everyone else did. Nothing was secret. She deliberately advertised her conquests in order to make them as widely known as possible."

"That's true, but nevertheless . . ."

The Russian stayed, so the Swede had to go off on his own.

To while away the time he decided to pursue his study of plant biology among the local flora. For this purpose he took with him on his rambles a syringe of morphia, as he wanted to see how plants reacted to this nerve poison, by means of which he hoped to prove that they had a sensitive nervous system.

One afternoon he sat down to enjoy a glass of wine in a garden restaurant on the outskirts of the village. Above his table hung the boughs of an apple-tree, laden with rosy fruit. This suited his purpose, so he climbed on to his chair, pierced the stem of an apple with his syringe, and pressed the nob, but too hard, for the apple fell!

At the same moment he heard a hue and cry from the slope leading to the wood, and saw a furious man, followed by his wife and children, come rushing towards him with upraised stick.

"Ha, ha, now I've caught him!"

Him? The man must mean a thief for whom he had been lying in wait.

Summoning all his Buddhism to his aid, he got off the chair and sat down, prepared to be carried off by a policeman as one caught red-handed. He saw no chance of being able to explain his behaviour, for no Prussian official would accept anything so bizarre as a person wanting to inject morphia into an apple-tree.

However, the angry man was delayed for a minute by a fence, along which he had to walk before he could get in.

The Swede sat like a doomed man and waited for a whack

from the stick by way of advance punishment. He was firmly determined to die like a warrior. He did not hasten to offer any useless excuses, but simply thought:

"This is the most fiendish thing that has ever happened to me in the whole of my wretched life."

Sixty seconds are a long time, but they too pass.

Whether it was his very well-cared-for and expensive suit, or the wine and the cigarettes of first-class quality, or whether it was something else that had a mollifying effect he did not know. But the angry man, who had certainly never before had such a grand customer, bared his head and merely asked if the gentleman had all he wanted.

He returned a polite answer, but noticed as he did so that the landlord was staring at the syringe, the box of powder, and the glass of water.

With the easy manner of a man of the world he began to explain how the unpleasant situation had arisen.

"I'm a botanist, and I was just about to carry out an experiment when I was surprised in a highly suspicious attitude."

"By all means, Professor, make yourself at home. You are free to do as you please."

After making a few remarks about the weather the landlord went indoors. His guest thought he heard him mumble something to the waitress, and this caused him to depart, but without appearing to hurry.

"He thought I was one of those mad people. That's what saved me. But I shall never be able to come here again."

The memory of those sixty seconds of humiliation, and of the raised stick, remained with him for hours afterwards.

"This is not bad luck, this is something else," was the conclusion he came to as usual.

His wife should have arrived that evening, but she did not come.

4

The Reunion

4

The Reunion

THE NEXT DAY he took his walk in the forest and brooded upon his fate.

"Why haven't you shot yourself? Why indeed? Because all your difficulties finally resolve themselves, and experience has shown that in the end things work out well."

This was what was called hope, and with it you warped your way along, moved up a pawl in the capstan and strode forward half a yard. Other people maintained that curiosity kept you going. You wanted to see how things would turn out, exactly as you do when you read a novel or see a play. He had not found that life had any purpose. It was true that religion taught us that we were here on earth to be improved, but he had only seen people being forced into situations out of which they emerged worse than before. Certainly it made you more tolerant of your fellow man, but this tolerance bore a close resemblance to moral laxity, for if you got as far as smiling indulgently at the crimes of others, you were not far from committing some crime yourself. When the talk turned on love, and people told him he should love his fellows, he summed up his views in the following words: "I neither love them nor hate them. I put up with them as they put up with me."

The thing that prevented him from ever becoming wholly overcome by grief was a dim feeling that life was not quite real, that it was a dream state, and that our actions, even the basest of them, were performed under the influence of a strongly hypnotic force outside ourselves. For this reason he did not feel himself to be entirely responsible. He did not deny the bad in himself, but he knew that, deep down, there was an upward-striving spirit that suffered humiliation at being clothed in human flesh. This inner personality had a sensitive conscience, which, to his dismay, sometimes pushed its way to the fore, turned sentimental and wept over his baseness, or its own, it was difficult to establish which. Then the one would laugh at the other's folly, and this was what he meant by "divine light-heartedness", which saved him more effectively than mournful rootling in misery.

When he got home he found his door locked. Guessing the reason he knocked and said his name. When the door was opened he found his wild young wife's arms round his neck, which seemed to him just as natural and just as understandable as if he had only left her for two minutes. Happy, younger and more beautiful than ever, she was his again. Not a word of reproach, of enquiry, or of explanation was uttered, simply: "Have you lots of money or only a little?"

"Why do you ask?"

"Because I've got lots, and I want to celebrate by dining in Berlin."

On this they were agreed; and such was their reunion. And why not? Two months of torture were forgotten, effaced, as if they had never been. The disgrace of a possible, and already rumoured, divorce had gone up in smoke.

"If anyone were to ask me what it was we quarrelled about," he said, "I should not be able to remember."

"Nor I! But that's why we must never, never part again. Never be away from each other for half a day. If we are, everything will go wrong again."

These were words of wisdom, he agreed, but . . . hm! Here a memory from Heligoland popped up, and then one from London, places where they had not been parted for a single minute, and where, for that very reason, things had gone utterly wrong. But he did not want to be petty.

"Just think, I've had my first royalties from Italy. Fifty lire! That poverty-stricken nation, with its enormous national debt, has sent me money. We must of course go to *Cantina Italiana* and repay the debt."

His wife too had good news. A play of his had been accepted at the Hofburg Theatre in Vienna.

"We have father to thank for that!"

"Oh, the kind old man!"

"Yes, do you know, he liked you so much that I was jealous."

"So I noticed! But tell me, what sort of a reception did you get?"

"Well, I don't want to talk about it! But it was all for your sake, so I forgave him."

And they laughed, even at *that*, and at everything else too.

"Right then, play today and work tomorrow!"

Autumn gave them what spring had promised but not fulfilled. They lived in a pleasant boarding-house, high up it is true, but with a view over the Schiffbauerdam and the Spree. Each in their own sphere had pleasant contact with former friends, so there was no longer any question of a perpetual *tête à tête*. The sun shone, an income was forthcoming, and life was easy to live.

This lasted for two months, two unforgettable months without a cloud. Unbounded trust, not a trace of jealousy. He spoke severely to her once when, out of pure mischief, she tried to make him jealous.

"Don't trifle with madness! If you play that sort of game you can be sure you will only arouse my repugnance. I shall hate you the minute you insert the image of a man into my conception of you."

But she was jealous, and envious too, even of his male friends, and Ilmarinen she simply drove away. If he spoke to the ladies who joined them at mealtimes in their boarding-house, she became indisposed and left the table.

She had no grounds for suspecting him of being unfaithful, but her desire to dominate was so overwhelming that she could not bear him to communicate his ideas to anyone, male or female.

Once, when settling some business with publishers on his behalf, she overstepped the limits of her authority, and instead of acting as his assistant, she behaved like his guardian.

"Remember what I said to you. If you abuse the power I've given you, I shall overthrow you as I would a tyrant."

He did not doubt her good will, but her lack of knowledge, and her high opinion of the extent of her own abilities, occasioned him embarrassment, even financial loss. But if he deprived her of her mandate she behaved like a naughty child, made a muddle of things and then threw them up, declaring they were worthless.

The ground was therefore prepared for what was to come.

One Sunday morning they had a tiff, as it happened on an important subject. As a result he locked the door between their two rooms. He then left the house. When he returned he found a written message from his wife to say that she had gone out into the country to visit a family she knew, and would be back that evening. In order to let her have a taste of what it was like to be alone, he made arrangements to spend the evening with some friends. The evening came, he went out, but towards ten o'clock thought it was cruel to stay out longer and returned home.

When he tried his door he found it was locked from inside.

"Ha, ha," he thought, "this is a plot! She means to force me into listening to a bedside sermon in her room."

He rang for the chambermaid.

"Is my wife at home?"

"No, sir, the lady came home at nine o'clock and went out again to meet you."

"Good, please open the door to her room."

She did so, but the door into his room was locked, as he himself had locked it that morning.

He then decided how to play his hand. He locked the door into the corridor and took possession of her room.

After a while came a knock from his young wife, and he answered through the locked door:

"You can have my room. I only hope you can get into it."

When she was unable to open the door all kinds of strange ideas came into her head. In her rage she decided that he was shut up with a woman, but would not of course admit that such an insult was possible, so sent for the police, alleging that a thief had been in the room and might still be there.

The police arrived. The husband got dressed and let them in, and they broke open the door between the rooms. Someone opened the door into the corridor at the same time.

A maid thought she had heard footsteps in the room, and when they got in they found a chair standing in front of the open window, so placed that it looked as if someone had mounted it in order to climb out on the roof.

Obviously a thief (or a woman) had escaped that way.

The police climbed out on to the roof with lamps and candles, and the male inmates of the boarding-house followed them. A shadow cast by a chimney moved.

"There he is!" someone shouted.

The police announced that they were not trained to climb over a steep slate roof and advised sending for the Fire Brigade.

"But that would cost fifty marks!"

The young wife signed a guaranty which the husband tore up.

Meanwhile a crowd had assembled in the street and neighbouring roofs were full of people.

A shout was heard:

"Here he is!"

They had seized an apprentice, who had joined forces with the besiegers with the worthy object of catching the thief.

A maid remembered that a visitor, who had arrived that afternoon, was now sleeping in an attic room next door. He might easily have got into the rooms.

The police forced their way into the man's room, inspected his identity papers, and found nothing.

All the attics were searched without result.

At midnight the police departed.

When they had gone the young wife wanted to embark on a series of explanations, but her husband was tired of the whole mad business and had nothing to explain. As he was given no choice, he carried his wife into her room and locked the door on her for the second time that day!

This diabolical incident was never cleared up. The husband did not believe there had ever been a thief, for nothing was missing from their rooms. He felt sure that his wife, who often went to the theatre, had pushed something into the lock, as had been done in *A Grey Hair*, and that, in the later stages of the comedy, demons had taken a hand.

He did not bother to find out what his young wife thought, for had he done so he would only have got caught in a tangle of fibs. He therefore drew a line through the whole business and the next morning they were just as good friends as before, though perhaps things were not quite what they had been.

No one has ever really explained what causes dissension between married couples. They love each other, are only happy in each other's company, have no differences of opinion, and suffer if they are parted. The whole of their combined egotism tells them to keep the peace, because strife between them is the thing that makes them suffer most. All the same a wisp of cloud appears, no one knows from where. All virtues turn into vices, beauty becomes ugliness, they face each other like hissing serpents, wish each other far, far away, regardless of the fact that they know that if they are separated for a moment, they will begin to experience the pangs of loss, and will suffer greater misery than any other that life has to offer.

Physiology and psychology run aground here. Swedenborg in his *Amore Conjugali* is perhaps the only person who has come near to solving the problem, but even he recognized from the start that to do so you have to employ high-powered equations which are unknown to the majority.

So it is that a man and wife, who love each other, may sit for an eternity wondering why they hate each other; that is to say, why they fly from each other despite the fact that they seek each other. Couples with an elementary knowledge of Ganot's physics might no doubt compare themselves to electrified balls of elder-pith, but they would not be any the wiser for that, nor any the happier.

Love has all the symptoms of insanity. Hallucinations, or seeing beauty where none exists. Melancholia of the deepest dye, alternating with boisterous merriment, and nothing in between. Unreasoning hatred, distorted ideas about the other's intentions (the so-called misunderstandings); attacks of persecution mania, during which they suspect the other partner of spying on them, of setting traps for them, of hounding them, why even of seeking to take their life, especially by means of poison. There are deep reasons for all these things, and the question is whether through living together, partners are not capable of clearly understanding each other's evil thoughts even before they are fully developed, and of believing them to have entered the region of consciousness with the firm intention of trying to become deeds.

Hardly anything hurts a person more than having another person reading their inmost thoughts, and this is something that

only married couples can do. They have no chance to conceal
the dark places of their souls, and they always seem to have
advance notice of each other's intentions. For this reason they
easily come to feel that they are spying on one another, which
indeed they are. Thus they fear no eyes so much as those of
their partner, for against each other they are defenceless. They
discover that they have at their side a judge who judges the
evil desire germinating within them while it is still a seed, and
yet no one is held responsible to the civil law for their thoughts.
Thus it would seem that in marriage we have a relationship
which stands a step higher than everyday life, which makes
more extensive claims and more exacting demands, and which
operates into the bargain with spiritual faculties that are more
finely developed. This is no doubt why the Christian church
has made marriage a sacrament, and regards it as a scorching
little furnace, not a bed of roses. Swedenborg's explanations
seem to lead us to the same conclusion.

Husband and wife may agree, but they are not allowed to go
on agreeing. When they try to gather roses they are made to
prick themselves on thorns as a punishment. The words *Omnia
vincit amor* mean that the power of love is so boundless, that if it
were allowed to run rampant it would be a danger to the
present order of things. Therefore, as it is a crime to be happy,
happiness must be punished.

Our light-hearted madcaps must have suspected this, for
when they had disagreed, they always made it up without
entering into explanations or reasons, as if they knew they were
not to blame for their quarrel, and that it was some other,
unknown being who had brought confusion into their lives.

So it was this time, but peace did not last for long. A few
days later an indisputable fact was established, which in normal
marriages is accepted as something inevitable, though feelings
may be mixed. Here it was received with marked disgust, and
the wife was beside herself.

"Now you have ruined my career. Now I shall be degraded to the status of wet-nurse, and what are we going to live on, I wonder?"

A feeling of personal dislike for the husband was aroused in her, and it rapidly degenerated into hatred. She was the independent woman, holding forth about what she believed to be the injustice of nature in allotting to woman all the discomfort, forgetting that her brief period of agony is followed by a supreme and long-lasting delight, which is for ever denied to men.

Of course no rational arguments were of any avail, and when the situation ceased to be ridiculous it became serious. Their scenes assumed an air of tragedy, and in the midst of all this he was prosecuted for his latest book, and the book itself was confiscated.

Autumn advanced and the absence of the sun was very noticeable. They felt cramped in the once happy attic, now transformed into a perpetually untidy sick-room.

Her hatred grew more and more intense. She could not go to parties or to the theatre, she could hardly go into the street. What annoyed her most was that the doctor—who had been summoned to diagnose a fatal disease, hitherto unknown—only smiled, prescribed soda-water, and said that all was as it should be.

Instead of having an understanding friend at his side he had a naughty, spoiled, and unreasonable child, and he longed to escape from his miserable situation. They no longer spoke to each other, but communicated solely by scribbling notes on scraps of paper.

There is a form of wickedness which is called meanness or iniquity and is difficult to define, but easy to recognize. It is the primitive evil in man, the positive desire to injure for no reason, and has not the justification of revenge or retaliation. It is very hard to forgive.

One day he got a scrap of paper on which was written something which made him give up going to her room. On top of that came her final declaration: she was returning next day to her family.

"Happy journey!" was his rejoinder.

Next morning, while it was still dark, he saw a white figure standing beside his bed. It stretched out its arms, as if pleading for forgivenness. He did not move, but let the figure stand. It fell to the ground, and he let it lie like an overturned statue.

From where did this tender-hearted man, who was always ready to forgive, get this determination, this inhuman severity? He did not know, but it seemed to him that it was imposed from without, like a duty, or an ordeal through which he must pass.

He fell asleep again, woke, dressed himself and went into the empty room. There he became aware of the vacuum. Everything was irretrievably over! Over!

His blood seemed to be flowing from opened veins; life was ebbing away, slowly but surely. And then came remorse for not having forgiven her.

Some violent upheaval was now needed to bring his ego to the surface again. He decided to drain a cup that in bitterness exceeded all others. He would go back to his country where he was damned by all.

When the steamer was half-way between Stralsund and Malmö he wrote a last letter to the captain and went up on deck with his revolver, intending to make the Baltic his grave. His Baltic. . . .

The reason he did not carry out his resolve? Yes, indeed, explain that if you can!

In the end he found himself in an hotel in a small town. But why should it have been just the town in which Laïs's relations and female friends lived, and where they were the leading set in the circles in which he was obliged to mix? He could only explain this as meanness on the part of fate, for in the matter of Laïs he was blameless.

All the same there he was in a hornet's nest, in an alien and enemy environment, and for three days he asked himself: "What business have you to be here?" And answered: "Here or elsewhere, what business have you to be anywhere?" So he stayed.

For three days and three nights he asked himself: "What is the point of staying alive?" Asked: "Where, whence, whither?" And all the time the revolver lying on the table was his answer.

Hamburg, London, Rügen, all began to shine as bright memories compared with this place of exile. It was so horrible that he began to marvel at the ingenuity of fate in devising torture chambers in which the terror steadily increased. His hotel room was an incitement to suicide. In other words it was a combination of gloom, discomfort and horror, and the same old conviction returned: "It's here I shall have to end my days."

His ability to hope was exhausted. He was slipping down into the empty void, which was beginning to close round him like the ultimate darkness.

On the fourth day he received a letter from his sister-in-law with the news that his little wife was well, and the suggestion that he and she should spend the winter in a little town in Moravia, an hour's journey from Vienna. His wife's relations would then be able from time to time to give her the help and advice of which, under present circumstances, she stood so much in need. Etc.

It was not all over! He had suffered these death-pangs for nothing, for he had not needed them to teach him to miss her. It was not all over! Life had been given back to him!

It should be mentioned as evidence of how completely extinct he had been that, during these days, a newspaper had printed an announcement that he was dead. He had sent off a humorous rejoinder, in the style of one writing from the gallows.

His torment was prolonged by three more days during which he was obliged to run round begging money for the journey.

5

The Year of Rejoicing

WHEN AT LAST the train stopped at the little station of the provincial capital of Moravia the first thing he saw was his wife's face, marked by suffering it was true, but transfigured by the radiance that motherhood bestows. When she caught sight of him her whole face lighted up as if a ray of sunshine had fallen on it.

"She loves me!" he told himself.

And life returned to him, literally, not figuratively.

"Are you happy?" he asked, almost shyly.

"Yes, now I'm happy," she whispered, burrowing her nose into the large pelerine of his coat and then kissing its hem.

"Whatever are you doing? Whatever are you doing?"

She hid her head under his coat to conceal her emotion, a thing of which she was always ashamed.

They had rented a two-roomed flat, a very shabby place. One of the rooms was dark and the better one was not pleasant, as it looked out on the industrial part of the town. His wife spent her time in the kitchen. She was resigned to her fate, for her maternal feelings were beginning to quicken, though they had not yet burst into full bloom. He did not like to see her drudging all day long, busy at the range or at the sink, and sometimes he was oppressed by a feeling of guilt. If he offered to carry something heavy for her she refused to let him, for she was absolutely determined that he should not be seen doing woman's work, nor could she endure the feeling that he was looking after her or doing her any little service. The storm had blown itself out. A great calm prevailed, and day followed day, all of them alike. They saw no one but each other, and had no social life or entertainment.

Then came poverty. The lawsuit against him had frightened publishers and theatres, and worst of all, he could not write!

What he could have written he would not write, for the subject matter concerned a family to whom he owed gratitude. But now, when he was about to have two families to support, he trembled at the thought of the future with its added responsibilities for, though he had long been aware of an increasing distaste for his calling as a writer, this distaste had now become abhorrence.

What an occupation! To sit and flay your fellow men and then offer their skins for sale and expect them to buy them. To be like a hunter, who in his need chops off his dog's tail, and after eating the flesh himself, offers the dog the bones, his own bones. To spy out people's secrets, betray your best friend's birthmark, use your wife as an experimental rabbit, behave like a Croat, chop down, defile, and burn, and sell. Fie, for shame!

In his despair he sat down to write up from his notes a survey of the relationship of chemical elements to reagents, believing, or in his need imagining, that by this work he would be able to find his way to a new career in science, the one on which he had embarked in his youth, before he became a writer.

His wife knew what he was writing, knew too that it would not bring in any money, but she controlled herself. Perhaps his burning faith had convinced her that there was something in it. She never complained; on the contrary, she encouraged him and offered to translate what he wrote into German.

A month passed, quietly, peacefully, but dismally. They knew that they were not enough for each other alone, in a solitary tête-à-tête. It grieved them, but they did not seek the company of other people. He, with his greater experience, pinned his

hopes on the arrival of the child, which would be the natural
source of company that would satisfy them both.

Meanwhile, poverty had marched closer. No plays were
performed, nothing was sold, not one of the hopes they had had
in the spring materialized. The children of his first marriage
were clamouring for money, and they began to be short of
food. They were rescued by an invitation to spend the winter
on a country estate that belonged to his wife's grandparents.

One December evening they got off a train at a little station
on the south bank of the Danube, and drove in a carriage along
its banks, through forests and untouched country.

It was all so new and strange. He was going to live in a house
in a curious relationship, that of a grandchild, whereas last
summer he had spent a week in a family as a child.

They reached the ferry at dusk. Ice had begun to form, the
river was also low, and there was a sandbank in the middle of it
where a fresh boat was waiting. From this point they could see
a large, white building, three storeys high, which looked
unfriendly, almost weird, with its projecting wings and tall
windows, ablaze with lights.

They landed, and he was very soon inside his haunted castle,
and being led along white-washed staircases, adorned by oil-
paintings with coal-black frames. He then found himself
standing in a warm, bright hall, in the midst of relatives, all
unknown to him with the exception of his mother-in-law.

With his usual incredible mental agility he entered into his
role immediately, and behaved like a young kinsman, whose
duty it was to show respect for his elderly relatives under all
circumstances.

His right to determine his own actions while indoors now
came to an end. He was obliged to fall in with the likes,
decisions, and habits of other people. In order to spare himself
unpleasant experiences he had made up his mind in advance
not to have any likes of his own, but to like everything

that came along, however alien and repulsive it might be.

The old grandfather was a lawyer who had retired with a large fortune, and had only turned farmer in order to supply his own household and because he enjoyed it. Most of his estate was a hunting-ground, and the whole property had fallen into a state of decay which town-dwellers think is picturesque. Both he and his wife were over seventy. They seemed to be living only in anticipation of their end, but with the happy resignation of the serene, unquestioning, orthodox Catholic. They had already built in their garden a mausoleum, in which they would finally rest, and they showed it off much as other people show off their country cottage. The building itself was a little white-washed chapel, round which flowers were planted and tended, as if the place was already a memorial.

In the house there was a surplus of the good things of this world and, after their period of half-starvation in Moravia, it was a question here of avoiding gormandizing without hurting anyone's feelings. Pheasants, hares, venison were the daily fare, and became in the end a punishment.

"This serves us right for complaining of manna. Now like the murmuring children of Israel, we shall have to eat quails until they stick in our throats."

A period of calm ensued, the calm of old age, free of all cares, all anxieties, in a house where the servants were as numerous as those they served. The old people, who had grown away from all interests, all opinions, and all passions, were easy to live with, and the young people, who had their own flat, were only expected to appear at mealtimes.

The young wife had now completely accepted the role of mother-to-be. She was full of hope and rejoicing, and talked of and to the unborn child as if she already knew it. She was gentle and feminine, even submissive, and grateful to her husband whose own feelings were unchanged, in spite of her misshapen figure and faded beauty.

"Is life a joy to you?" she asked.

"Yes, it is, but how long will it remain so?"

"Hush!"

"I will, but you too know that happiness is punished!"

No one asked him what he was doing. On the contrary, the only thing they said was: "You must do nothing, you must rest after the wild hunt you've been through."

He therefore sent for his scientific apparatus, which a rich man had given him two years previously, and which he had been forced to leave behind in his native land. He then started on a series of systematic investigations and carried out experiments which he wrote up. He felt new life and greater interest beginning to stir in him and when, by means of syntheses and analysis, he saw his former hypotheses and calculations verified, he became convinced that he was working with a reliable method, and along the right lines. This gave him enough confidence to feel that his work was justified, but since he could not explain the meaning of his researches to the uninitiated, his position was insecure. People had to take him on trust, and this they were prepared to do so long as peace reigned, but at the very first hint of antipathy, he would be helplessly at the mercy of the ridicule or pity of the people about him.

The old grandfather, a great huntsman and fisherman, was a close observer of nature, and had also studied natural science. He was therefore curious about what was going on upstairs in the flat. When he asked questions he received evasive answers, but as he had been a judge and a barrister he insisted on clarification. When he was told of the nature of the investigations, he shot them down on the authority of the textbooks. In order to bring the futile dispute to an end his young relative let him think he was right, but the old man first provoked him into refutations, and then assumed a haughty expression and became impertinent, which for the time being he was allowed to be.

"Nothing for nothing" was Axel B's view, and his wife thanked him for being accommodating, and praised his self-control. But it had been written that there should be discord, and discord there was.

The prosecution in Berlin had repercussions beyond the confines of Germany, and one day an officer of the law arrived with a summons calling upon the accused to go for interrogation to the nearest town.

Right from the beginning he had challenged the competence of the Court in Berlin, for he held that a Swedish author was under no obligation to answer to a Prussian Court for a translation of his work. He therefore had reason to regard the whole prosecution as illegal, which it was, and he refused to attend the hearing. The old gentleman, on the other hand, stuck to it that he must appear before the judge, chiefly perhaps because he did not want to have the police in and out of his house.

In order to put an end to the affair Axel B decided one morning that he really would go to the court to register his challenge.

He set off at about eight o'clock and walked along the beautiful road beside the Danube. But when he had got half-way he met a postman who gave him a c.o.d. package which contained a long-expected sheet of palladium.

The fact was that while analysing sulphur he had found that this substance, which was regarded as an element, contained carbon. He had deduced by analogy that to extract the carbon he must extinguish the flame with a sheet of palladium, which would precipitate carbon separated into very fine particles.

A sheet of palladium was more costly than gold, and as he had no money, he had to devise some other means of obtaining it.

After brooding for a month he had remembered that he had a chest of valuables which was deposited at a place in the north of Sweden. He therefore wrote to a friend and asked him to sell the things for a sum corresponding to the price of a sheet of palladium. His friend was then to change the money into Austrian currency, and send it in an unregistered envelope, so that no one would know what had been done. He regarded the transaction as a theft from his wife and children, but a theft that he must commit, as it would enable him to solve such an important problem.

When he held this longed-for piece of equipment in his hand his soul caught fire, and without hesitation he turned back home.

"Hurrah! Now I'll strike my blow. Once that's done the police can come when they please."

When he got home the old gentleman was standing in the courtyard cutting up a roebuck that he had shot. Axel B tried to make himself invisible, but did not succeed.

"Hello, have you been to the judge already?" asked the old man suspiciously.

"No," answered the defaulter brutally, and slipping into the house he ran upstairs into his room and bolted the door.

He then got the sulphur ready in a crucible, having previously lit the spirit-lamp that would heat it.

"In half an hour," he said to himself, "the greatest problem of modern times will be solved."

There was a knock on the door.

The moment to light the sulphur had arrived.

The knock was repeated, loudly, determinedly.

He would have to open the door to get any peace. He opened it.

"Why didn't you go to the judge?"

"That's no business of yours!" was the answer, and the door was banged to like a shot.

But his peace was at an end. He could hear voices down below, and he knew that his fortunes had changed. His hand shook, he became as it were paralysed and extinguished the lamp, for at that moment he had also lost faith in what he was doing, and did not dare to risk a failure.

After two minutes his mother-in-law came in. She was not angry, but she was embarrassed by having to convey the news that he and his wife must leave that very day before dinner. They could have her little one-storey house that lay beyond the garden, and could fetch their food from the big house.

His little wife came in dancing with joy because they were to have a house of their own, and especially that house, with its own garden and park.

The move took place and now, just as spring was approaching, the two most delightful months of their life together began.

Their cottage, built of grey stone, was completely idyllic. The minute windows had sandstone surrounds and wrought-iron gratings. It looked like a monastic building and its walls were clad with vines. Inside the walls were white-washed and unpapered, and the low ceilings had sturdy beams, black with age. He had been allotted a little room the shape of a real monk's cell, long and narrow, with a tiny window in one of the end walls. These walls were a yard thick, and for that reason he could have flowers both inside and outside the windows. The furniture was old-fashioned in keeping with the rest.

Here he established his laboratory and his library, and felt more at home than ever before.

To prepare it for the arrival of their child they decided to furbish the place up. Husband and wife painted window-frames and doors. Roses and clematis were planted by the entrance. The garden was dug and seeds were sown and, in order to fill up the large expanse of white walls, he painted pictures.

When all was finished they sat down to admire the work of their hands.

"Isn't it lovely! Now we're ready for our little one."

"Think how pleased she'll be to see so many pictures on her very first day!"

"Yes, but you mustn't smoke her out with sulphur."

"I'll sell my sheet of palladium and buy her a horse and carriage, complete with an outrider and a footman."

They waited and hoped. On long spring evenings they talked of nothing but her (or him), tried to guess which it would be, discussed names and speculated about its future. The wife's thoughts turned most to the question of whether she would be fair, and like his son, whom she loved.

Both she and her family had a strange passion for fair-haired people, but whether it was because they resembled the light, while dark people reminded them of darkness, it was difficult to say. They thought well of all fair people, and spoke ill of Jews, regardless of the fact that his little wife's paternal grandmother had been a Jewess. On her mother's side of the family, which stemmed from a race of Bohemian farmers, the word "Jew" was used as a term of abuse. His father-in-law too was anti-semitic, but when Axel B suggested jokingly that this seemed to be rather bizarre, his wife answered:

"You mustn't joke about it. Only we are allowed to do that."

At last one day in May, when the sun was shining, the unknown traveller announced his arrival, and after twelve frightful hours turned out to be a girl, but at least she was not dark.

This should have made the idyll perfect, but instead it appeared to have brought it to an end.

The little one did not seem to feel at home in this vale of tears, for she screamed night and day. Wet-nurses were engaged and wet-nurses were dismissed. The little house was filled with five women, who all had differing views on the subject of child-care. The father went about like a criminal and always seemed to be in the way. His wife thought she had noticed that he did not seem to love his child, and this wounded her so deeply that he too became upset at the sight of her distress.

Her own transformation was complete, she was now a mother and nothing else. She put the child in her own bed, and was capable of spending the larger part of the night sitting on a chair lost in admiration of the beautiful sleeper. Sometimes he was called in to admire too, but at such moments it was the mother who appeared to him most beautiful. She had forgotten herself and, with a blissful smile on her face, she sat absorbed in contemplation of her child.

But rough weather began to blow up from outside too. The local people were very religious, and the child's incessant crying was giving rise to talk. People were asking if it had been christened.

By law a child should adopt its father's religion, but as both he and his wife were rather indifferent, they thought the christening was unimportant and put it off, especially as there was no Protestant clergyman anywhere near.

The child's screaming was certainly not normal, and when the local people began to give vent to their opinions, the mother-in-law came to them and insisted that it must be christened:

"People are muttering, and they have already threatened to stone your house!"

The irreligious young couple did not believe her, they simply smiled. But the muttering increased. A peasant woman had seen the devil in the garden, and the foreign gentleman was dubbed a "Swedish heretic". Some grounds for the rumours about local feeling there must have been, for people who met the "heretic" in the road crossed themselves.

Finally an ultimatum arrived from the elderly relatives:

"The child must be christened within twenty-four hours or you will all be sent across the Danube."

In other words: "Cast out the bondwoman and her son."

To this he answered: "We Protestants are fairly tolerant

about our faith, but when this is made a question of money, we are as fanatical as any Catholics!"

The position was threatening, for the young couple had not a farthing with which to finance a journey. His letter was answered with a straightforward: "Then out you go!"

"To be martyrized for a faith you don't hold is certainly rather bizarre. I never expected that we should have to enact the Thirty Years War again down here. But beware all of you. The Swede is coming, and he's going to carry off his daughter in his baggage-wagon, for she's a Swedish subject."

The imperial party in the great house, who had begun to waver, now decided to try what stratagem could do.

The child was declared to be ill. It grew sicker each day, and finally the great-grandmother arrived with her retinue and informed the child's father that the little one had not long to live.

He did not believe her. But the next day after a long walk in the woods, his wife met him on his return with the news that the child had received private baptism from its nurse in the presence of the doctor.

"Into which faith was the child baptized?" asked the father.

"Into the Protestant faith, of course."

"But I don't see how a Catholic nurse could perform a Protestant baptism."

However, seeing that his wife was in the plot, he said no more.

The following day the child was well, and nothing more was said about turning them out. The imperial party had won.

"Jesuits!"

The child, who had been expected to bind the couple still closer to each other, seemed to have come to divide them.

The wife thought her husband showed no interest in the little thing.

"You don't love your child!"

"Yes I do, but like a father. You love her like a mother. That's the difference."

The truth was that he was afraid of becoming attached to the new-born child. He had realized that he and her mother were going to part, he could feel it in the air, and under those circumstances, to be tied to his wife through the child would be like being in shackles.

She on her side didn't quite know what she wanted. If he loved the child he might take it from her when he went. If he did not love it he would simply leave them, for she had a premonition he would go.

The fact was that a play of his had been a theatrical success in Paris that spring, and that another play was billed for the autumn. He wanted to go there of course, and she wanted to go with him. But the child restricted her movements, and she felt sure that if he went alone, she would never see him again.

Letters bearing French stamps now began to arrive frequently, and this aroused her curiosity, especially as he immediately burnt them.

This last circumstance was so contrary to his usual habits, that it provided her with an excuse for suspicion and hatred.

"You're planning a journey, aren't you?" she said one vening.

"Of course I am," he answered. "I can't live in this state of uncertainty, never knowing whether or not I'm going to be turned out on the high road."

"You're thinking of leaving us, I suppose?"

"I must leave you if I'm to settle my affairs in Paris. But making a business journey doesn't mean I'm abandoning you."

"In that case you can go," she snapped, thereby betraying herself.

"I shall go as soon as the money I'm expecting arrives."

At this the fury appeared on the scene again. First of all he was made to move up into an attic room. Then, regardless of the fact that she and the child were already occupying two rooms, she deliberately dismantled the third room, which was their dining-room, and particularly charmingly furnished. She tore down the curtains, stowed away the pictures and lumbered up the whole place with baby-clothes and milk bottles, simply in order to show who was master in the house. The rooms all looked as if demons had run riot. Food, kitchen utensils, and baby-clothes were strewn over beds and sofas.

On top of this she served up evil-smelling or burnt food, and one day she put before him a plate of bones that looked as if the dog had been gnawing them. With them she gave him a decanter of water. This last was an expression of the greatest disdain, for the cellars were full of vats of must, and you could not get servants unless you promised them must with their meals. His position therefore was lower than that of the servants.

He suffered in silence, for he knew that the money for his journey would arrive. This did not prevent his loathing from mounting as high as her hatred.

He was now living in the midst of dirt, want, and spite, hearing only squabbling and shouting between his wife and the nurse, his wife and the maid, his wife and her mother, while the child screamed all the time.

Then he fell ill with a fever and a throat infection, and had to stay in bed in his attic. She did not believe he was ill, and let him lie.

On the third day he sent for a doctor, as he was unable even to swallow water. Then his fury appeared at his door:

"Have you sent for a doctor? Do you know what that costs?"

"It will be cheaper than a funeral at any rate, and besides, it may be diphtheria, which would be a danger to the child."

"Do you mean to say you've actually thought of the child?"

"Yes, a little."

Ec

If she could have consigned him to the Danube she would have done so. As it was she simply treated him like one suffering from the plague. The child, the child was in danger!

"I've lived through many things," he said in a whisper, "but I've never experienced evil as great as this in anyone."

And he wept, perhaps for the first time for twenty years, wept over the misery of it all, and perhaps too over his own bad luck and humiliation.

Looked at objectively it seemed to him utterly unnatural that he, an eminent man in his profession, should, through no fault of his own, be living so wretchedly that even the maid pitied him. Since he had arrived at the home of his relatives his behaviour had been irreproachable. He had never got drunk, for the simple reason that there was nothing to drink. He had also had theatrical successes in Italy and in Paris, but instead of helping him by increasing people's respect, as successes that come the way of normal mortals usually do, these had only served to aggravate their hatred and affected disdain.

He did not feel obliged to allow the fact that he had accepted hospitality from these immensely rich relatives to weigh upon him, for was he not the lawful heir to half of all they possessed? But now that hatred was on the rampage they soon made him understand what he cost them, and even suggested payment.

Once again he became obsessed by the old idea that things were not taking their natural course, but that on the contrary, an invisible hand was controlling his fate.

He even thought that the inexplicable non-arrival of the money for his journey had been specially arranged in order to prolong his misery.

When other expected letters did not turn up, he began to suspect that the cause originated with his wife. He therefore started to spy on the post bag that the ferryman brought, and to send communications to the post-office, with no result of course except ignominy.

Though he was an unbeliever a sort of religious crisis came upon him. He felt he was being degraded by circumstances in which material things predominated, circumstances where the animal side of things, food and excrement, took a prominent place in the conversation, where wet-nurses were treated like milch-cows, circumstances which were full of cooks and rotting vegetables and the discussion and exhibition of physical phenomena which we usually conceal. To make things worse a downpour had put a passage and a couple of rooms under water, and this could not be got out, but was left where it was to stink. The garden too fell into decay now that he no longer tended it.

He longed to get out, to get away, but far away, to light and cleanliness, to peace and love and reconciliation. He began to dream his old dream of a monastery, within whose walls he would find shelter from the temptations and filth of this world, a place where he would be able to forget and be forgotten. But faith was lacking, and the ability to obey.

This idea of a monastery had long haunted literature, and he and his friends in Berlin had talked of founding a non-confessional monastery for intellectuals who, at a time when industry and finance had pushed themselves so much to the fore, could not feel at home in the atmosphere of a materialism which they themselves had been misled into preaching. He now wrote to a friend in Paris about the founding of such a monastery. He sketched out plans for the building, drew up rules and went into details of the communal life and duties of the brothers. This was in August 1894! The aim of this monastery was to be the training of supermen, by means of asceticism, meditation and the practice of science, literature and art. Religion was not mentioned, since he did not know what religion there would be, or whether there would be any religion at all.

His wife noticed that her hold on him was loosening, but she believed that his thoughts were turning to Paris, with its vanities and amusements, its theatres and cafés, its romantic adventures, and its thirst for gold, and she both feared and envied his thoughts. Her scorn and ridicule on the subject of his scientific studies had vanished since he had received encouraging letters both from an eminent German authority and from a famous Frenchman, letters which, to protect himself, he had felt obliged to show her. But, as she could no longer criticize his ideas, she moved the battle over to another square, and began to plague him with sly questions about how much he earned by his chemistry.

On top of that she egged on a doctor member of the family to question and browbeat him. Old women too came and asked him if he would soon be making gold. His wife herself disarranged some apparatus he had under observation, thereby destroying the work of many days.

When she was angry she would betray all the little and big secrets that a wife and husband share between them, and repeat things he had said about the old people in moments of irritation. She regretted this afterwards, but by then it was too late. The damage had been done and the storm could no longer be controlled.

If he had any money, and was bold enough to offer to contribute to the household expenses, she was horrified that he could be so coarse as to suggest paying rich relations for their hospitality. If he had no money she came along with obvious jeremiads about how dear everything was and sent him the doctor's bill. In a word: the unpredictable moods of an undisciplined person were something against which it was impossible to fight.

He often thought of going on foot to Vienna to seek out some fellow-countryman, who would help him on the next lap of his journey. But every time he set out he turned back as if he were bewitched, or fettered to the little promontory on which the cottage stood. He had had happy times there, and the memory of them held him captive. He was drawn there too by gratitude for the past, and by love for the child which he felt, but dared not show as, had he done so, the child would have become the lime-twig to which his wings would have fastened.

One day he had been for a long walk over the glorious *Auen*, or water-meadows, where deer frolicked, where pheasants rose from the bushes like rockets, their bright metallic plumage gleaming like a rain of stars, where herons fished in the marshes, and golden orioles whistled in the poplars. He loved being in this place, for it was a waste-land where no human being had dared to put his dwelling for fear of the great floods.

He had now walked there alone every morning for three-quarters of a year. Not even his wife was allowed to go with him, for he wanted to keep this bit of country to himself, to see it only with his own eyes, to hear in it no other human voice, so that when he revisited it no memory would be awakened of any other person than himself.

Thus in this place he was able to regain his own personality, to find himself and no one else. Here his great thoughts came to him, here he performed his devotions. The inexplicable happenings of the past months and his deep suffering had made him change the word Fate to Providence, thereby indicating that a conscious, personified being was directing his life. In order to have a label of some sort he now called himself a Providentialist. In other words: he believed in God without being able to define what he meant by that word.

Today his emotions were shot with melancholy. It was as if he were saying farewell to these meadows and thickets. Something was at hand, he suspected what it was, and he also feared it.

On returning home he found the house empty. His wife had gone; the child had gone.

When the maid finally appeared and he asked her what had happened to his wife, she answered saucily:

"Madame has gone."

"Where?"

"To Munich."

He did not know whether to believe her or not. All he knew was that the silence and emptiness gave him great pleasure. He breathed uncontaminated air, he delighted in the solitude, and sat down to work with the indestructible calm of a Buddhist. His bag was already packed, and he expected the money for his journey to arrive that day.

The afternoon passed. When he looked out of his window he noticed that the great house looked unusually peaceful; none of the relatives were visible. On the other hand his maid was running backwards and forwards, as if she were taking reports. Once she had come in and asked if there was anything he needed.

He had answered that there was nothing, and this was the truth, for his only wish had been to be quit of all the mess and muddle, and this wish was now granted without his having to take any steps about it. He ate his supper alone and enjoyed doing so. He went on sitting at the table and began to smoke. His soul took up that happy position on the scales from which it could come down on whichever side it pleased. He was careful not to wish anything, for fear of seeing his wish crossed, but he expected something.

"If I know anything about women they won't be able to sleep tonight until they've sent a deputy to find out whether the victim is suffering as they expect."

And true enough, his mother-in-law appeared.

"Good evening," she said. "You're all alone here, my son."

With the calm of an Indian facing the fire that is going to roast him he replied:

"Yes, I'm here alone."

"And what do you propose to do?"

"Go away, of course."

"You seem to be taking it all very calmly."

"And why not?"

"Maria is going to ask for a divorce."

"I can well believe it!"

"Then you don't love her!"

"You wish I did, for then I should really and truly suffer."

"Can you suffer, I wonder?"

"You'd be pleased if I could."

"When are you thinking of leaving?"

"As soon as I get money for the journey."

"You've been saying that for a long time."

"You're not proposing to turn me out on the high-road tonight, are you?"

"Grandmother is very annoyed."

"Then tell her to pay attention to what she's doing when she says her prayers tonight."

"Goodness! One gets nowhere with you."

"No, why should I allow you to?"

"Goodnight to you!"

And with that she departed.

He slept well and soundly, as if something which he had been expecting for a long time had happened.

When he woke the following morning he found himself thinking: "She's not gone. She's somewhere in the neighbourhood."

And when he went outside he saw the maid going off in the ferry-boat with some equipment that belonged to the child.

"Ha, ha! Now I know. She's somewhere on the opposite bank."

The maid soon returned, but not before he had had time to watch her manœuvres on the other side through binoculars.

"If only we keep calm now," he thought, "the imperial party will be defeated."

His mother-in-law arrived. She looked uncomfortable, but kind.

"Yes, my son, now you're alone. You'll never see her again."

"Is she so far away then?"

"Yes, of course!"

That made him laugh, and he looked meaningly towards the other side of the river.

"Ah well," said the old lady. "Since you know, go after her!"

"No, I'm not going to do that."

"She won't be the first to come."

"First or last, it's all the same to me."

The boat plied backwards and forwards with reports all day. In the afternoon his mother-in-law appeared again.

"You must make the first move," she said. "Maria is beside herself, and she'll fall ill if you don't write to her and ask her to come back."

"How do you know that I want her back? A wife who spends a night away from home has forfeited her marital rights and wounded her husband's honour."

This was an unexpected riposte. His mother-in-law hurried off, had herself put across the river, and was away the whole evening.

He was sitting in his room writing when his wife came in. The expression on her face seemed to say that she had taken pity on his sufferings, and come back in answer to his insistent entreaties.

He could now have crushed her, but he did not do so out of generosity towards the defeated.

When he found himself with a wife and child in the house once more, he felt pleased, just as pleased as he had been when they were away, perhaps on the whole rather more so.

That evening the money for his journey arrived. This put him in an entirely different position, for he now held the key to his prison-house.

His wife now began to look at the matter from another angle. "You must see that this life is killing me. I haven't read a book since the child arrived, and I haven't written anything for a year. I shall go to Paris with you."

"Let me go first and spy out the land."

"That will mean I shall never get away."

He persuaded her to stay. It was not that he had any definite plan for leaving her. He simply wanted to feel free to start with.

She on the other hand, though she called her child the most important person, was quite willing to leave it if by doing so she could get away and play some part in the world. She knew very well that he was not leaving her to seek his fortune, not knowing what that would be, but to harvest the fruits of a success already achieved. So the ambitious and independent woman had risen to the surface again, perhaps also the jealous rival, for there were moments when she conducted herself as the superior author. This happened when she had received letters from women friends telling her that she was a genius, letters which she left lying about for him to read.

Fortunately she was prevented by the old people from taking this opportunity of getting away. They put a stop to it, and she resigned herself to the fact that he must leave her by regarding him as a person who was being driven away. She became gentle, affectionate and emotional, and their parting was quite painful.

And so he went out into the world again. As the steamer chugged its way upstream on a lovely autumn evening, he saw once more the little house, the lights twinkling from its windows. All the evil and ugliness he had known there was obliterated, and he was only faintly aware of a fleeting feeling of joy at being quit of the prison in which he had suffered so terribly.

Only feelings of gratitude and tenderness now held him in their grip, and at one moment the ties that bound him to his wife and child pulled so hard that he thought of throwing himself into the water. Then a few strong turns of the paddle-wheels pushed the boat forward, his bonds tautened, lengthened, and broke.

Commentary and
Notes

ON 29 OCTOBER 1898, Strindberg wrote to his friend Gustaf af Geijerstam at the publishing firm of Gernandt as follows: "In eight days I shall probably have finished the first part of my novel, 350 pages of it, so arranged that they can be served up by themselves as a whole book if necessary."

On 23 November he sent the completed manuscript with these words:

"Herewith the first part of *The Cloister*, which is only an introduction.

"Please do not allow any unauthorized person to read it!

"You'll understand that I'm sending it for financial reasons.

"It's worth a thousand kronor, even if I die, because it can be served up on its own.

"Let me have the money as soon as you can! My young are screeching, and I with them!

"*The Cloister* must not be published until April, and it may be that I shall knock off a play in between!

"Anyone who wants to know the story of my life should read in the following order:

The Son of a Servant
Time of Ferment
In the Red Room
A Madman's Defence
The Cloister Part I
Inferno
Legends
The Cloister Part II"

The Cloister Part II was never written. *The Cloister Part I* is primarily the story of Strindberg's second marriage to the beautiful young Austrian journalist, Frida Uhl, entered on when she was twenty and he was forty-three.

The title refers to a café in Berlin, close to Unter den Linden, called *Das Kloster*, but renamed by Strindberg *Zum schwarzen Ferkel*, the Black Boar. This café, and some of the people who frequented it, played an important part in Strindberg's life at the time he met Frida Uhl. It was the haunt of artists, actors and writers, and soon after he arrived in Berlin, Strindberg became a member of one of the bohemian coteries that had made it their headquarters. The group of gifted people that he joined, and upon whom he exercised a great influence, has come to be known as the "Ferkel Circle". Most of its members were Scandinavian exiles like himself, but several were German, and one was Polish.

Notes on the men and the one woman of this circle who are mentioned in *The Cloister* will be found at the end of this book.

While he was still thinking of writing Part II of *The Cloister* Strindberg was anxious to stress that, when using the words as the title of his book, he had something more in mind than the café. On 4 November 1898 he wrote to Geijerstam:

"Don't imagine that by *The Cloister* I only mean the café, and that the whole book will deal solely with our revels there. Chance has ordained that the café really is called *The Cloister*, so I have let it stand. The second part of the book will deal with the real cloister, and with my personal impressions of Maredsous rearranged."

Maredsous was a Benedictine monastery in Belgium, not far from Dinant, in which Strindberg had spent one night in August 1898. He had several times toyed with the idea of retreating into a monastery, but had never actually taken this step, perhaps because to have done so would have involved "a profession of faith and obedience, which I hate," as he wrote to a friend in 1895. The night he spent in Maredsous seems to have been the only occasion on which he actually stayed in a monastery.

More important than the fleeting attraction Catholicism had for him was the idea of a serene and disciplined society, a non-confessional body of intellectuals, the object of which was to be: "the training of supermen, by means of asceticism, meditation, and the practice of science, literature, and art," as he tells us in Chapter 5 of *The Cloister*. This idea recurs in others of his works, most notably in *To Damascus* Part III, and in *Black Banners*.

Strindberg tells us that he and his friends in Berlin had discussed this project, but the picture he gives of them, and of the life they led at the Cloister, seems very far removed from the monastery of his dreams. The orgies in which he and his friends indulged were no doubt the outcome of their state of mind. The Scandinavians among them, Strindberg says, were men who were "dissatisfied and at loggerheads with the people at home," and who had come to Berlin to seek "recognition, understanding and daily bread". These were precisely his own reasons for being there.

The circumstances under which Strindberg had left Sweden were, even for him, peculiarly unhappy. In 1891–2 he had passed through the nerve-racking experience of the divorce proceedings between him and his first wife, Siri von Essen, to whom he had been married for fourteen years. The court had awarded her the custody of their three children, and this had been a bitter blow to Strindberg who, whatever his failings as a husband, was and always remained a devoted and affectionate father.

He was desperately poor. His countrymen, who had never appreciated his outstanding qualities as an author, had now turned definitely against him. In Sweden his plays were not performed, and his books were not printed. He had no money with which to pay his debts and support his children, and he had to live largely on the charity of his friends.

In 1892 Strindberg wrote no fewer than seven plays, among them *The Bond* and *Playing with Fire*, but they were all refused. *The Bond* and *Playing with Fire* were not even printed until 1897. No wonder he wrote no more plays for six years.

His plight was well known, but though he was clearly the most outstanding writer Sweden had produced, he was not awarded any State or public stipend—as Ibsen was in Norway —to help him in his hour of need.

From this situation he was rescued by fellow-countrymen and friends who had already moved to Berlin. The money to get him out of Sweden was raised by private subscription, and he arrived in Berlin on 1 October 1892.

His name was already known in Germany. A number of his plays had been translated and published, but only two, *The Father* and *Miss Julie* had been performed, the latter only once. Now the energetic wife of one of his friends set to work to get others translated and, as we read in *The Cloister*, soon after his arrival one of his plays was performed. This was *Creditors*, which was put on at the Residenz Theatre on 22 January 1893. The Manager of the theatre was Siegmund Lautenburg, the man to whose party Strindberg had refused to go, without knowing why he did so. His conversation with the Manager on this subject, at the celebration party, is recounted in *The Cloister*. What he fails to tell us is that Lautenburg, in an access of enthusiasm, told him that he might expect 30,000 marks in royalties. The play was a success, but Strindberg never got the money. Eventually Lautenburg offered to buy the play outright for 3,000 marks, an offer which the author indignantly refused. This caused a break with Lautenburg, who declined to perform *The Comrades* as he had promised. Things of this sort not infrequently happened to Strindberg, who seems to have been very unequal to managing his business affairs himself, but very touchy if anyone else tried to do so.

On the whole things went tolerably well for Strindberg in Berlin, but he seems to have been quite willing to accept Frida's suggestion that he should try his luck in London. The foundations upon which he and Frida based their hopes of getting a foothold there were flimsy to say the least of it. The one indisputable fact was that Justin Huntly McCarthy had twice publicized Strindberg in England; once in an article on some of his plays, which had been published in the *Fortnightly Review* of September 1892, and once in a translation of part of Strindberg's own Preface to *Miss Julie*, which had appeared in the *Gentleman's Magazine* of August 1892.

When they arrived in London in the spring of 1893, they found that the rumours that a play was to be performed were untrue. These may have emanated from J. T. Grein, the person upon whom their one visit was paid. He was a Dutchman living in London, who had started an experimental theatre, the Independent Theatre, on the French and German models. He had contacted Strindberg early in 1893, while the latter was in Berlin, and said that he intended to produce *The Father*.

However, when they met him in London Grein told them that it was too late to produce the play that year. He did, however, suggest that if they wanted to move into central London from Gravesend, where they had first taken lodgings, they could use his house in Warwick Street, Pimlico. This was the scene of their London battles. According to Frida Strindberg did not enjoy living in Grein's house, and found the food provided by Grein's housekeeper abominable. He could, however, just manage to take his meals at J. T. Grein's table and sleep in J. T. Grein's bed, but to work at J. T. Grein's desk, "at which someone had sat fighting with his whole soul for Ibsen," was impossible. Ibsen, Frida tells us, was the stumbling-block in Strindberg's path in London as elsewhere.

The publisher, whom rumour had reported to have a book ready for the press, was Heinemann, Ibsen's publisher, and he flatly refused to handle anything by Strindberg.

The fateful book that Frida read in London, and that had such a disastrous effect upon their relationship, was *A Madman's Defence* (*Plaidoyer d'un fou*), written by Strindberg in French, but first published in German under the title of *Die Beichte eines Thoren*, in May 1893. It is the novel which he mentions having sold "for quite a considerable sum" just before he married Frida. He had received a thousand marks as advance payment.

This book was to cause him further trouble. In the autumn of 1893 Strindberg was prosecuted in Berlin for writing an indecent and immoral work. This was the prosecution that "had repercussions beyond the confines of Germany," and caused the row with his wife's maternal grandfather, which is described in Chapter 5 of *The Cloister*. He was finally acquitted in 1895, but it is clear that the prosecution was a shattering blow to his morale, and may well have increased his aversion for his profession, and made him all the more determined to pursue his scientific studies.

Even the theatrical success in Paris, which he gives as his reason for leaving Frida and the child, was not enough to divert him from his scientific studies, or discoveries, as he himself called them. This success was the performance of *Creditors* at the Théâtre de l'Œuvre on 21 June 1894. It was followed by a performance of *The Father* at the same theatre on 15 December 1894.

But his success in Paris brought him neither money nor happiness. For the next two years he lived in great poverty and distress, writing articles in French, many of them of a pseudo-scientific or frankly alchemistic nature.

By 1896 the climate of opinion in Sweden was beginning to change. Strindberg's *Lucky Peter's Travels* was put on in the autumn of that year in Stockholm, and ran for sixty-five performances.

At the beginning of December 1896 Strindberg returned to Lund for a time and wrote *Inferno* there in May and June 1897, but he wrote it in French, as he was still very uncertain of finding a publisher in Sweden. As it happened a Swedish translation of the book was published by Gernandts in October 1897, before the original French version, and was followed in 1898 by *Legends*, most of it also written in French, but only published in Swedish.

It is clear from the things he wrote to his publisher Geijerstam, at Gernandts, that he was very nervous about the reception these autobiographical works would receive. When he heard that all was well he wrote: "So no putting me away, no prosecution."

In the plays *To Damascus*, Parts I and II, 1898, he was again using material garnered from his own experiences, but this time he wrote in Swedish. After them he wrote *The Cloister* Part I, also in Swedish.

As we have seen, *The Cloister* Part II was never written, and Part I was not published during Strindberg's lifetime in its original form. C. G. Bjurström thinks this may have been due to its "blatantly autobiographical character, involving as it did not only Strindberg and his second wife, Frida Uhl, but also the whole of the group from *Zum schwarzen Ferkel*."

Whatever the reason, *The Cloister* Part I lay unused until 1902, when Strindberg revised the work and published it under the title of *The Quarantine Officer's Second Story* (*Karantänmästarns andra berättelse*) in a volume of short stories and poems entitled *Fair Haven and Foul Strand* (*Fagervik and Skamsund*).

When revising the story Strindberg tried to disguise its autobiographical nature, but he did this carelessly and in haste, and his efforts left the work in a somewhat mangled condition. It is therefore highly satisfactory that, thanks to C. G.

Bjurström, we are now able to read it in its original form.

A letter of 8 September 1902 to Geijerstam seems to indicate that Strindberg himself was not entirely satisfied that the changes he had made would effectively disguise the story. "When you have had time to consider the contents of my new book," he wrote, "we ought to discuss whether it does not need a little collection of poetry (now ready) to act as rearguard cover for the Quarantine Officer's rather dangerous story. (previously *The Cloister*, now set in Denmark)."

The scenes in the original story were laid in Berlin, Heligoland, England, and Austria, and the chief characters retained their true nationality: the hero was a Swede, and his wife and her parents were Austrian. In *The Quarantine Officer's Second Story* all this was changed. Berlin became Copenhagen, Heligoland an island in the English Channel off Dover, England remained England, but Mondsee was changed to Arreskovsjøn near Odense, and Maria's grandparents are said to live not by the Danube, but in the interior of Jutland.

The nationality of the characters too was changed (though not their names). The hero became a Norwegian, and his wife and her family Danish. Neither this change nor that of location was carried through to its logical conclusion. The names of the places were changed, but the description of the scenery was not, and as there is little resemblance between Austria and Denmark the result was incongruous. The characters too have a habit of reverting to their original nationality. When she reveals the fact that she knows about Axel's affair with Laïs, the Danish Maria still exclaims in German "Wer dreiundzwanzig Jahr alt ist der weiss Alles!" (If you're twenty-three you know everything.)

Another important change that Strindberg made was in the nature of Axel's secret occupation. In *The Quarantine Officer's Story* he was still a writer and a dramatist, but his other occupation which, in the revised story, he did not keep secret from his wife, was not scientific investigation, but a historical treatise. Strindberg was careless about this alteration too, but it did cause him to change or delete a number of passages which throw much light on what he was doing and thinking in 1893-4.

For instance, the whole of the passage early in Chapter 3 which begins: "He had begun to be interested in chemistry and the other natural sciences even in his early youth," and ends: "he kept the matter a secret from his wife," was deleted, and in Chapter 5, after the row with his wife's grandfather over his failure to appear before the Judge, the whole of the telling passage which begins: "But his peace was at an end," and finishes, "he had lost faith in what he was doing and dared not risk a failure," a passage which reveals Strindberg's doubts about his scientific work, loses its point when the words "extinguished the lamp" are replaced by "shut the book".

On the other hand the Axel of *The Quarantine Officer's Story* was still making botanical experiments, so the absurd encounter with the angry man who suspected him of wanting to steal his apples was left as in *The Cloister*.

The switch from science to history makes it difficult to understand why the local people in Dornach should have regarded his occupations with suspicion. There is nothing particularly odd about a man who reads books, but a man who insists on turning a room in a cottage into a laboratory, who carries out strange experiments, and makes nasty smells is an entirely different matter. In *The Quarantine Officer's Story* the passage "Old women came to ask him if he would soon be making gold" was changed to "Old women came to question him", but we are never told about what.

When Strindberg was making his alterations he had before him a manuscript of 314 pages. Of these he removed pp. 1-54, and pasted over p. 55, except for the last three lines. He then added a new introduction and an epilogue, in order to fit the story into the framework of the Quarantine Officer's two stories.

On the piece of paper pasted over p. 55 of the original manuscript Strindberg wrote the last lines of his new introduction.

The lines left uncovered at the bottom of p. 55 are those which begin: "The author's theatrical successes began to be expressed in terms of invitations . . ." early on in Chapter 2. This then is where Strindberg began to make his alteration: i.e. to change the old story *The Cloister*, into the new story *The Quarantine Officer's Second Story*.

This manuscript, which we may call Manuscript B, came into the possession of a certain Arvid Ulrick, who refused to allow John Landquist to see it in 1920, when the latter was working on the volume containing the story in his complete edition of Strindberg's collected works. Landquist was therefore obliged to reprint *The Quarantine Officer's Second Story* from the printed version of 1902.

The first fifty-four pages, which Strindberg removed, represented the whole of Chapter 1 and Chapter 2 of *The Cloister* as far as the words: "most of the others had already caught a glimpse of her in the street." These pages will be referred to as Manuscript A.

This manuscript was discovered after Strindberg's death and published separately by Professor Carlheim-Gyllensköld in *Samlade Otryckta Skrifter* (*Collected Unpublished Works*, 1919), under the title of *The Cloister*.

Both Manuscript A and Manuscript B are now in the Royal Library in Stockholm. In 1951 Professor Walter Berendsohn published an article in *Samlaren*, in which he showed that when the sheet pasted over p. 55 was removed, the two manuscripts together form the whole of the original manuscript of *The Cloister* except for the last page which is missing. Manuscript B comes to an end at the words: "and she resigned herself to

the fact. . . ." We cannot therefore be absolutely certain how
The Cloister ended. In the Swedish edition C. G. Bjurström has
used the ending of *The Quarantine Officer's Second Story*, as he
considers that this makes a perfectly fitting conclusion to *The
Cloister*.

This is certainly true if the work is regarded as fiction, but
if we take it to represent part of Strindberg's autobiography, it
does not tell the whole story. He and Frida did not part for ever
by the banks of the Danube. She joined him in Paris in September 1894, and they spent two eventful months together.
Strindberg never mentioned these months except in letters, but
he described their final parting in *Inferno*. "It was with feelings
of savage glee that I returned homewards from the Gare du
Nord, where I had parted from my little wife. . . . Her last
words 'When shall we meet again?' and my answer 'Soon,'
still echoed in my ears like an untruth. . . . Those farewell words
that we exchanged in November 1894 were in fact our last, for
up to the present time, May 1897, I have never seen my dear
wife again."

However, in spite of its rather misleading ending, *The
Cloister* remains an important autobiographical source. C. G.
Bjurström first published a French translation (*L'Abbaye*,
Mercure de France 1965), but it is from the Swedish edition,
(*Klostret*, Bonniers 1966) that my translation has been made.

The principle that C. G. Bjurström followed when preparing
the Swedish edition was this: in places where Strindberg had
altered or deleted words and passages in order to disguise the
autobiographical character of the work, he returned to the
original 1898 version, and gave the 1902 version in a note. On
the other hand where the changes that Strindberg made in
1902 represented an improvement in style, these were allowed
to stand, and the original version was given in a note. These
notes have been omitted in the present edition, as they are
only of interest to Swedish readers.

Regarded as a work of art *The Cloister* does not rank very high among Strindberg's works. He used the material of his second marriage and his *Inferno* crisis to better effect in his plays *To Damascus* I and II, and in *Advent*, a play which he first intended to call *The Mausoleum*, and which was a bitter attack on his wife's maternal grandparents in Dornach. But as an autobiographical source *The Cloister* is invaluable, not only for the light it sheds on his second marriage, and the vivid picture it gives us of his second wife, but also because of what it tells us of his attitude, in 1898, to the people and events of 1893–4.

The very factor that makes the book less effective as a work of art makes it all the more trustworthy as an autobiographical document. Although in it Strindberg not infrequently complains that something or other is the most fiendish thing that ever happened to him, he seldom seems to work himself up into the white heat in which he composed most of his best work. I feel myself that in *The Cloister* he is looking back on the events of 1893–4 with a certain detachment, and at times with some amusement.

Even in 1894 his attitude to his marriage had been, for him, unemotional. In the autumn of that year when, soon after he had arrived in Paris, he and Frida were debating by post whether she should join him there, or he return to Dornach he wrote: "Remember what I once said: a bad marriage is better than no marriage at all. It's too quiet here. No one to plague me, or make me angry. I long for a real, honest quarrel, from which you would unquestionably emerge the master." And later, in November, after Frida had left him because their child was ill, he wrote to his friend Richard Bergh: "I don't really know much about my marriage. I never took it very seriously, as you probably noticed in Berlin, and it is most likely breaking up—I can't say for certain. At times it was very amusing and satisfactory, but language, race, ideas of right and wrong, and bad habits often stretched it to the limit."

This was the man who could adopt the ruse of taking to his bed, and posing as sick, in order to divert Frida from making an unpleasant scene; who could talk of "divine levity" and "blessed light-heartedness" which "saved him more effectively than mournful rootling in misery." The man who could stand aside and look at what was happening to him objectively, and say of it: "If I don't come out of this with honour, I shall at least get a chapter for my novel."

At the same time we meet in *The Cloister* the Strindberg of 1898, the man who had endured the severe mental and emotional upheaval of the *Inferno* crisis, and who saw the hand of fate, or of some other unseen power in everything; who could write that he and Frida "were not to blame for their quarrel, as some other unseen being had brought confusion into their lives," and who could also "marvel at the ingenuity of fate in devising torture chambers in which the terror steadily increased." The man who could not believe that things were taking their natural course, but that "an invisible hand was controlling his fate."

Even the occasion when he seems to have changed his mind, and calls himself a "Providentialist, a man who believed in God without being able to define what he meant by that word," reminds us of the Strindberg of 1897, who could write in *Inferno*: "I thanked Providence, which had sent me to that despised little town, there to atone for my sins and find salvation."

The other matter of major interest on which *The Cloister* sheds light is Strindberg's attitude to his so-called scientific studies. That he had a genuine interest in science is indisputable, but whether he really believed himself to be capable of solving the problems he tackled is another matter. It is clear both from *The Cloister*, and from some of his letters of this time, that he was well aware that the ground on which he was treading was far from firm. He needed the encouragement and confirmation of recognized authorities to give him confidence. He consulted other people—a thing he would never have dreamt of doing in matters of literature—and we can see from his letters that he classified his friends as "believers" and "unbelievers", and that he was greatly depressed because many of them belonged to the latter category.

The question is, was he always a believer himself? The passage in Chapter 5 where he speaks of himself "believing, or in his need imagining" that he could find a new career in science is very revealing.

After the row with his wife's grandfather we read that: "His hand shook, he became as it were paralysed and extinguished the lamp, for at that moment he had lost faith in what he was doing, and did not dare to risk a failure." This was the man who in *Inferno* could write: "I was assailed by doubts about my scientific investigations. Suppose they were pure folly? Alas! If so I had sacrificed a life of happiness for myself, and for my wife and child too, all for a chimera."

We have doubts about the life of happiness, but we can have none in thinking that by abandoning his profession as a writer and turning to science, which under the influence of the Paris occultists became alchemy, Strindberg did something which had a disastrous effect upon his mental health.

What was it that drove him to turn from his proper occupation as a creative writer just at the time he had achieved a European reputation as a dramatist?

Professor Berendsohn is surely right in thinking that the prosecution in Berlin of his book *A Madman's Defence* had a profound effect upon his attitude to his own writings. Strindberg himself confirms this view in the passage in Chapter 5 of *The Cloister* where he bursts out: "What an occupation! To sit and flay your fellow men and then offer their skins for sale, and expect them to buy them . . ."

But for Strindberg, to give up writing drama, fiction and

verse was to deprive himself of his own greatest safety-valve, his mental and emotional therapy, and for this purpose the works that came from his pen during the years 1894–7 were no substitute. Most of them were of a scientific or alchemistic nature, and almost all were written in French. In spite of his proficiency in this language, to write in it, and in a sphere in which he was not an acknowledged master, cannot have given him the same satisfaction and relief that he found in writing Swedish literature.

He himself has recorded in *Alone* (*Ensam*, 1903) the nature of this satisfaction. He has been out on his morning walk, sometimes a harmonious, sometimes a disharmonious experience, and he writes:

"When I get home and settle down at my desk, then I really live, and the energy I have gathered out-of-doors, whether it comes from the broken circuit of disharmony, or from the closed circuit of harmony, is now made to serve my various purposes. I live, and I live multifariously all the lives of the people I describe. I am happy with the happy, evil with the evil, good with the good. I creep out of my own person and speak from the mouth of a child, of a woman, of an old man. I am a king or a beggar, I am a man set up on high, a tyrant, I am also the most despised, the oppressed, the hater of tyrants. I hold all kinds of opinions, profess all religions, I live in all periods and I myself cease to exist. This is a state that brings with it indescribable joy."

But the Swedes had plainly shown by their hostility and neglect that they had no use for him or his writings. As Gunnar Ollén has pointed out in his book *Strindbergs Dramatik*, of the twenty-five plays he had written by 1892, only *Master Olof* and *Lucky Peter's Travels* had given him any financial return worth mentioning, and many of his best plays remained unperformed in Sweden.

It seems to me probable that the achievement of a European

reputation did not in any way make up to him for the neglect he suffered in his own country, and that the feeling of being persecuted and exiled played an important part in the mental and spiritual upheaval of the years 1894–6.

But in 1896 his plays again began to be performed, and by 1897 a publisher was willing to allow an autobiographical work, *Inferno*, to appear in Swedish. It was in this atmosphere of reconciliation that the *The Cloister* was written, which may well account for its comparative lack of bitterness and vituperation.

Much of the material for this note has been gathered from C. G. Bjurström's Commentary to the Swedish edition of *The Cloister* and from Professor Berendsohn's admirable article in *Samlaren* 1951.

MARY SANDBACH

Notes

1 *A young Norwegian dramatist*, Gunnar Heiberg.

2 *A doctor*, Carl Ludwig Schleich, a surgeon with literary and artistic interests who frequented *Zum schwarzen Ferkel* and was one of the circle round Dagny Juel. He greatly admired Strindberg and helped him financially. He also encouraged him in his scientific studies, but more because he admired him for what he was, and what he had done, than because he believed in what he was trying to do.

Strindberg and he spent many hours together "mixing colours, devising chemical experiments, poring over the microscope, developing photographs, painting, making music, studying counterpoint, or what not," as Schleich himself tells us in the chapter on Strindberg in his autobiographical work, *Those Were Good Days*.

3 *Ilmarinen*, The Finnish-Swedish writer Adolf Paul. He must have been a man of some ability in spite of Strindberg's scornful reference to him as "this insignificant, uneducated Ilmarinen". He wrote successfully in both Swedish and German. In 1930 he published a spiteful book about Strindberg called *Min Strindbergsbok* (*My Book about Strindberg*, not translated), in which he gave his version of the Rügen visit and many other incidents in *The Cloister*. Paul says he went to Rügen to write and found Strindberg's demands on his time and sympathy an unmitigated nuisance.

The picture Paul gives of Rügen and the conditions there does not suggest that they were anything like as unpleasant as Strindberg would have us believe. What Paul has to say is a useful reminder that even in his autobiographical works Strindberg wrote to produce a desired effect. Two eyewitnesses agree that Strindberg made use of Paul, but they also make it clear that the latter was a distinctly unpleasant person. Edvard Munch calls him "a nauseating creature . . . who served as a doormat," and Jens Thiis, the Norwegian art historian, who met Strindberg and Paul in Berlin is equally outspoken. "Perhaps Strindberg had humiliated him, but his whole personality invited such treatment. There was something of the pariah about him. I could not endure him."

4 *The Russian* (also called Popoffsky), Stanislaw Przybyszewski. A gifted but erratic Polish author who was Strindberg's devoted friend and admirer until the breach over Dagny Juel. In 1891 he had entered into a so-called "free" marriage with a German girl by whom he had two children, but he abandoned her and in September 1893 married Dagny Juel (Laïs). To enhance the dramatic effect of his meeting with Popoffsky at Pankow in August, Strindberg pretends that the marriage had already taken place.

The breach with Przybyszewski and the whole business with Dagny Juel worried Strindberg a great deal. His letters of 1893–4 are full of references to them. As Popoffsky, Przybyszewski features large in *Inferno*. His signature tune there is Schumann's *Aufschwung*, and whenever Strindberg heard it being played he became convinced that "the Russian" had come to murder him out of jealousy.

In 1895 Munch painted a picture in Paris entitled "Jealousy" with a man's green face (Przybyszewski) in the foreground and another man gazing at a naked woman (Dagny Juel) in the background.

5 *The Savage*, Richard Dehmel, a German poet, who had himself studied economics and science and seems to have given Strindberg some encouragement in his scientific studies, but been sceptical about his conclusions. Strindberg's letters to Dehmel do not suggest that relations between them were ever like those described in *The Cloister* when Strindberg visited Dehmel at Pankow. In the same month (August) Dehmel was offering to put into poetic shape the rough translation Frida had made of Strind-

berg's poems *Sömngangarnätter* (*Somnambulist Nights*). Schleich's description of Dehmel suggests that he was quite capable of the frenzy ascribed to him by Strindberg in Chapter I of *The Cloister*.

6 *The Danish painter*, Edvard Munch, the well-known Norwegian painter. It is difficult to know why his nationality should have been disguised in *The Cloister*, but Strindberg had called him a Danish painter in *Inferno*, and simply continued the practice. He refers to him as a Norwegian painter in Chapter 2 of *The Cloister* when he is talking of the turmoil an exhibition of his paintings had caused in Berlin. Munch painted Strindberg's portrait in Berlin and also made a drawing of him at *Zum schwarzen Ferkel*. He also did a lithograph drawing of him in 1896 in Paris, which he labelled Strinberg (*sic*), and framed the head in a pattern of zigzag lines on one side, which merged into the seductive lines of a naked female body on the other. He explained this by saying he wanted to enclose Strindberg in lines representing masculine and feminine characteristics. Strindberg was not pleased.

Munch is a rather shadowy figure in *The Cloister*. He plays a more important role in *Inferno*.

7 *she's a painter*, Dagny Juel. Strindberg calls her Laïs in *The Cloister* and Aspasia in *Inferno*. She is an enigmatic character who seems to have exercised a fatal fascination over all the men with whom she came in contact. She was a Norwegian and was introduced to the Ferkel circle by Edvard Munch. As we see in the story she abandoned him for Strindberg, whose mistress she was for three weeks. She then transferred her affections to Bengt Lidforss and others, dropped them all temporarily and married Stanislaw Przybyszewski, Popoffsky of *The Cloister*. Lidforss reported to Strindberg that she had gone back to Munch, but Paul says that she left Przybyszewski for another Pole, who shot her when she was proposing to leave him for a third.

She is said to have had a "figure like a fourteenth-century

Madonna, and a laugh that drove men crazy. She could drink absinth by the litre and never get drunk." Clearly a woman whom it was not easy to forget, as Paul's description of her confirms. "A classically pure profile, the forehead concealed by a wealth of curls, so that you could estimate its height and its intelligence as you pleased. A smile that made you long for kisses, but at the same time inspired fear of the two pearly rows of sharp teeth, that lurked behind her thin lips as if waiting for a chance to strike. There was in addition a snake-like languor in all her movements, which nevertheless did not exclude the possibly of a lightning attack."

8 *An old friend of Läis's*, Bengt Lidforss. A distinguished Swedish botanist. In *The Cloister* Strindberg clearly means Lidforss when he talks of "the friend who was in love with her" (Laïs) and who was staying with Ilmarinen on Rügen. This is an invention on Strindberg's part. The friend was in fact K. A. Tavaststjerna, a Finn, who was very deaf, and therefore not particularly good company, but who does not appear to have been annoyed with Strindberg for having flirted with his newly-wedded wife when they were all three together in Weimar. However, Tavaststjerna would not have served the purpose of the story, which was to make Rügen appear a hell on earth.

Lidforss and Strindberg met in Lund in 1891 and became good friends. They had much in common, Strindberg was interested in botany and Lidforss in literature. They quarrelled over Dagny Juel in the spring of 1893, but by September were again exchanging friendly letters. In February 1894 Lidforss translated into German Strindberg's *Antibarbarus*, a work on scientific subjects written in Brunn, when he and Frida were living there in poverty before they moved to Dornach.

Lidforss occurs again in *Inferno*.

9 *His friend the Dane from* The Cloister, Holger Drachman, a Danish poet.